Off the Record

Center Point
Large Print

Also by Susan Page Davis and available from
Center Point Large Print:

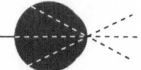

**This Large Print Book carries the
Seal of Approval of N.A.V.H.**

Off the Record

Susan Page Davis

CENTER POINT LARGE PRINT
THORNDIKE, MAINE

The text of this Large Print edition is unabridged.
In other aspects, this book may vary
from the original edition.
Printed in the United States of America
on permanent paper sourced using
environmentally responsible foresting methods.
Set in 16-point Times New Roman type.

ISBN: 978-1-63808-889-9

The Library of Congress has cataloged this record
under Library of Congress Control Number: 2023940403

Chapter 1

Wynne Harding clenched her teeth as she stabbed the computer keys. She'd worked at the newspaper office for three weeks, and she was getting used to the software her new employer used, but some of the formats were much more sophisticated than those she'd worked with at the small weekly paper in New Hampshire.

She wanted to make good here. She had to. But the new job was much harder than she'd imagined.

After snarling up her article about a proposed addition to the junior high school, she tried feverishly to untangle it without having to ask for help again. Julie Saxton, at the desk across the aisle, had been enthusiastically helpful, but the time had come for Wynne to figure this out on her own.

"Section break," she muttered.

"All right, crew," her immediate boss, Chuck Barnes called, and heads went up all over the room. "Somebody's been hurt in a farm accident in Belgrade. Who's going out there?"

Nobody answered, and Wynne's head whirled. She grew up in the small town of Belgrade, the tourist haven nestled amid several lakes. There were several working farms out there, but she wasn't sure she knew any of the owners. She'd moved away, with her parents, right after high school.

Julie, who tripled as copy editor, librarian, and paginator, frowned at him. "Chuck, you've only got two reporters here right now."

Jim Dowdy lifted his chin. "Not me. I've got the mayor's press conference in thirty minutes." As usual, Jim Dowdy felt his current project was too important to leave for something else that was probably smaller. Management seemed reluctant to push the *Guardian*'s prize-winning reporter. Scuttlebutt had it that Jim could hire on with any number of bigger papers.

Chuck's eyes swung around and landed on his rookie. "Looks like you're up, Wynne."

She flinched as panic rose in her throat. She hadn't been sent out solo on an accident yet, and she wasn't sure she could handle it emotionally, let alone ask the right questions at the scene.

When she glanced apprehensively at Chuck, he had already swiveled toward the other end of the newsroom. "Go with her, Ken."

Wynne took a deep breath and sent up a silent prayer of thanks. Ken Ricker was a veteran photographer. He had been friendly to her since her arrival in the office. He was fifty-eight, graying, and fatherly, and occasionally he ate lunch with her in the break room, telling stories about the old days when they still shot rolled film and developed it themselves.

Surely Ken had absorbed a lot of knowledge about news writing in his thirty-five years with the paper. She was especially grateful that the brash young photographer, Jerry, had not been tapped to go with her.

Ken approached her desk, plucking a piece of paper from Chuck's hand as he passed him. Wynne hastily gathered her purse, notebook and car keys.

"Want to take the company car?" he asked Wynne.

"That would be great, especially if you're driving." Though she could find her way to Belgrade without any trouble, she'd been away too long to remember all the local roads once they got there.

Ken led her down the stairs and out the back door to where a white compact car was parked. *Waterville Guardian* was stenciled in black on the door.

"Hop in." Ken opened the driver's door and slung his camera bag smoothly into the back seat.

On the way, Wynne scribbled a few notes in her thin reporter's notebook, trying to guess what the right questions were in a case like this.

"Nervous?" Ken asked.

"Kind of. Mostly, I've been writing up school news and features. I rode around with Jim one day, but I haven't covered an accident by myself."

"Don't worry about it. It may be all over by the time we get there."

"In which case, we do what?"

"Contact the state police, or whoever responded. Belgrade's too small to have its own police department. There's probably a county sheriff's deputy out there."

"I grew up out here." She watched the scenery fly past her window. So many new houses in the last five years.

"What part of Belgrade?" Ken asked. The town bounded several lakes and was divided roughly into three settlements—Belgrade Village, Belgrade Lakes, and North Belgrade, where they were now.

"Down toward the village," she said, "on the way to Belgrade Lakes."

"We're not going that far today."

She nodded. "Just so you know, I'm not so good with blood. Do we know what happened?"

Ken reached in his shirt pocket for the slip of paper Chuck had given him and handed it to Wynne. On it was scrawled, *Barton Road*, and under that, *Kid fell off tractor*.

"So a child was injured?"

"I don't know," Ken said. "Sounds like. Could have been run over by the tractor."

"It's not a fatality, is it?" She felt a little queasy.

"Don't know. Guess we'll find out soon."

Wynne couldn't remember where the Barton

8

Road was, but Ken had tapped the address into his phone and followed it through North Belgrade, toward Belgrade Village on the south side of town, toward Augusta.

"There it is." He swung the car to the right, onto Barton Road. Half a mile later, they spotted an ambulance and two police cars in the yard between a large, red barn and a neat, white Greek revival farmhouse.

Pulling in behind the nearest cruiser, Ken parked and stretched for his camera bag. Emergency medical technicians were fastening straps and tucking a blanket around a small form on a gurney outside the rear door of the ambulance.

Ken leaped from the car, camera in hand, leaving Wynne to do her own job. Her heart raced as she climbed out of the car.

A stocky sheriff's deputy watched from one side, and a state trooper was talking to a tall man in jeans and a red plaid shirt. Nearby, an elderly woman stood with her hand on the shoulder of a little boy who watched the EMTs soberly. The child on the stretcher was crying loudly, continuously.

Ken strode to the back of the ambulance and snapped a picture as the technicians positioned the gurney behind the vehicle.

"Just great!" The man in the flannel shirt turned angrily on Ken. "My daughter's going to the hospital and I've got reporters in my face."

Wynne timidly approached the deputy. "Excuse me, sir. I'm from the *Guardian*. Could you tell me what happened here?"

"Little girl fell off the tractor." He glanced at her, then back toward the ambulance.

"Uh, are you investigating, sir?"

"Nope. Dave Workman got here first."

"Is he the state trooper?"

He nodded curtly.

Wynne jotted the name on her pad and took a few steps toward the trooper. She stood quietly, wondering if she would dare speak to him.

"So, you riding with her?" Workman asked the child's father.

"Definitely." Lines of worry etched the father's face, and his troubled eyes stayed on the crying child. Wynne wondered if she should know him, from her schooldays in Belgrade. He was quite a bit older than her, and she decided he wouldn't have been in her social sphere. He'd probably graduated long before she entered high school.

"Go ahead," said Workman.

The man stayed close the gurney. One of the EMTs was telling the little girl, "It's okay, honey, you're going to be all right," but she didn't stop wailing long enough to hear it.

The father's face softened as he bent over and stroked her cheek. "Daddy's here, baby. It's okay."

As they lifted the gurney, Wynne could see that

the skin over the little girl's left eye was swollen and purple. Her wails became screams as she was hoisted into the vehicle.

The father stood waiting, his shoulders tense, as the EMTs settled her in the ambulance. When the patient was secured, one of the uniformed men stepped down. "You can get in now, sir."

The father turned abruptly to Ken. "I don't want a picture of my little girl in the paper. She fell. That's it. Are you hard up for news today?"

Wynne saw that the trooper was looking at her, his dark eyes shaded by the wide brim of his regulation hat. She seized the opportunity. "Excuse me, sir, can you tell me what happened?"

"The little girl was climbing on her father's tractor, and she fell off and landed on her head." Workman eyed her with undisguised speculation. "You from the Waterville paper?"

"Yes, sir."

"Never saw you around before."

"I just started. So, the tractor wasn't moving?"

"Nope, wasn't even running."

She wrote it down. "It came in as a farm accident at our office," she explained. "We didn't know what to expect."

The father turned, pausing with his foot on the step. "If you print this as a farm accident, I'll never hear the end of it. Why don't you just forget the whole thing?"

"I'm sorry, sir. It's my job." Wynne quaked as his intense blue eyes raked over her. A smear of grease smudged his forehead, where a damp lock of light brown hair drooped toward his right eyebrow. He was younger than she had realized, and he would have been handsome if his expression wasn't so belligerent. He's scared, she thought.

"If she fell off her bike would you print it?" he asked.

Wynne shrugged helplessly. "I'm sorry this happened to your daughter."

He stared at her for half a second then got into the ambulance, and the EMT closed the door. The little girl's muffled wails could still be heard until the engine started.

"Don't take it personal," Workman said. The ambulance pulled away, and he turned toward his car. "What else you need?"

Wynne fell into step beside him. "Well, names, for one thing."

Workman consulted the report form he had begun to fill out. "Hallee Cook, age four. The father's name is Andrew. She was climbing around on the tractor with her brother, just playing, and she slipped and fell off. The boy ran into the barn to get their father, and he sent the kid to the house to get Grandma to call 911."

Wynne wrote it all in her notebook, and Workman stood watching her. Out of the corner of her eye, she saw Ken striking up a conversation with the elderly woman.

"She'll likely be fine," she heard the woman say.

"And you're the investigating officer?" Wynne asked, just to be sure.

Workman snorted. "Not much to investigate." When she arched her eyebrows, he said, "Sure, sure. David Workman. State Police."

"And they're taking her to the hospital in Waterville?"

"No, the Alfond in Augusta."

"Oh, right. Any broken bones?"

"Didn't seem to be. Her eye was puffed up, and she had a little cut on her head. She wouldn't quit screaming long enough to tell the EMTs anything."

"So, as far as you know, just the head injury?"

"That's enough."

Wynne nodded soberly. "Anything else I should know?" It wasn't much of a story, and she was fishing.

"I don't know what. Andrew's right, though. If you bill this as a farm accident, he'll probably have social workers and aggie people out here bothering him. It was a kid accident, not a farm accident."

"Got it. Thanks." She closed her notebook.

Workman eyed her keenly for a moment, and Wynne felt the blood rushing to her cheeks. "You fresh out of high school?"

13

She didn't dignify that with a reply but turned away to where Ken was saying to the woman, "I'm sorry about all this, Mrs. Cook. I hope she'll be all right."

The woman turned toward Wynne. Her arm was still around the little boy's shoulders, the breeze ruffling her snowy hair. Her smooth cheeks were slightly rounded, and her hazel eyes were clear.

"My name is Wynne Harding."

Mrs. Cook nodded.

"I was sent out to write up the accident."

"I'm sorry my grandson was so short with you." She was gracious, even in crisis, smiling apologetically. "Andrew isn't usually like that. The EMT said Hallee might have a fractured skull, and that upset him."

Wynne's heart wrenched. "He must be terrified."

"Well, these kids are all he's got." Mrs. Cook's protective arm never left the boy's shoulders.

"You ought to be proud of the boy for being so quick and helping the way he did," Ken said.

Young Andy kicked at a rock with his toe.

"Thank you, I am," Mrs. Cook replied.

"How old are you, Andy?" Ken asked.

"Four."

"They're twins." Mrs. Cook gave then a wan smile. "I guess I'll take Andy in the house, in case Andrew calls from the hospital."

"Mrs. Cook, I'm sorry Ken and I had to come

out here and bother you folks," Wynne said sincerely. "If we'd known more about what happened, our boss probably wouldn't have sent us. If he makes me write it up, I'll try not to sensationalize it. And—I'll be praying for little Hallee."

Mrs. Cook's face melted from courtesy into warmth. "Bless you, dear. Thank you." She gave Andy's shoulder a squeeze and led him toward the house.

Wynne walked toward the car with Ken. She buckled her seat belt and sighed deeply. "Is it a non-story?"

"I don't know." Ken was thoughtful. "You could write a few inches, make the boy a minor hero."

"I don't think the family would like that." Wynne winced, remembering Andrew Cook's rage when Ken snapped the first picture. "Do we have to use a photo?"

Ken sighed. "I snapped one of Worden, in case Chuck insists. Just tell him it wasn't much and see what he says. I'll back you up, and I'll say we were too late for a picture of the little girl. Her father's right—we wouldn't run a story about a kid falling off a bike and cracking his skull."

Chapter 2

"Four inches," Chuck decreed. "We'll put it in a box on the split page."

"I doubt I can stretch it to that," Wynne protested. "It really isn't—"

"News is news." Chuck looked her over distastefully. "You've been here what, two weeks?"

"Three."

"Right. Let me decide what's news." He walked away, and Wynne sat down hard in her chair, her cheeks flaming.

"You got art for that, Ken?" she heard him yell.

"Nope."

"What?" Chuck was livid.

"They were already putting her in the ambulance when we got there."

"You coulda got a picture of the crummy tractor!"

Ken opened his mouth but closed it without saying anything.

Chuck shook his head and stalked out of the room.

Wynne opened a new file and began to type slowly. *BELGRADE—A four-year-old girl was injured Monday afternoon when she fell from her father's tractor in the yard of the family home on Barton Road.*

She reached for the telephone and called the hospital.

"Patient information, please." She was put on hold. She typed another sentence. *Hallee Cook and her brother were playing on the tractor when the mishap occurred.*

"May I help you?"

"Yes, this is Wynne Harding with the *Guardian*. A little girl named Hallee Cook was brought into the emergency room a little while ago. We'd like a status report on her, please."

"You know we can't give out patient information to anyone but family," the woman said.

Wynne hesitated. "Can you confirm that she's there?"

She was put on hold again. She looked at the second sentence of her story and added to it, *according to state trooper David Workman, the investigating officer.*

"I'm sorry, we don't have an admission report for Sally Cook."

"It's Hallee. With an H."

"One moment, please."

Wynne sighed and pecked out another sentence telling which ambulance company had responded and the name of the hospital.

"Sorry, ma'am. No admission record for the Cook girl. She could still be in the E.R." The

18

woman hung up, and Wynne replaced the receiver and stared at her monitor screen, hating the story and her own helplessness.

She looked over at Julie. "The hospital won't tell me anything about the patient. What do I do?"

"You could ask someone in the family, I guess. If it was a police case, they could tell you." Julie got up and walked down the aisle between the workstations, heading for the library.

Wynne plodded on through her story, typing carefully so she wouldn't hit extra keys by accident, inadvertently reformatting the entire piece. She was determined not to call Julie back from the library to help her.

At the next desk, copy editor Esther Dart sat frowning at her own computer screen and murmuring, "Where'd you go? I know you're in the system."

Two more reporters sat on the other side of the four-foot dividers. Jim Dowdy had returned from the mayor's office and was typing rapidly, while Scott Therien, a sports reporter who had the luxury of coming into the office later than most of them, talked loudly on the phone.

"You're kidding!" Scott laughed. "You're the third coach to quit this year. Is it the referees?"

Wynne closed the file on Hallee Cook and opened the article she had been working on when Chuck sent her to Belgrade. She tried to shut out Scott's chatter and concentrate.

She reviewed what she had written about the new addition at the junior high school and thought about where she wanted to go with the story. The words flowed in her mind, but the mechanics of getting them onto the screen were a trial. She had thought she was a good typist until she came to the *Guardian* and tried to adjust to the confusing array of function buttons on their keyboards.

Julie's phone rang, but she was still in the library, so it went on ringing. Wynne glanced toward the desk where Karen, the receptionist, usually fielded calls, but Karen was nowhere to be seen. On the fifth ring, Wynne answered it on her own phone.

"*Waterville Guardian*, Wynne Harding speaking."

"This is Bud Hallowell. Is Julie in?"

Wynne's adrenaline ran riot as she recognized the name of the newspaper's publisher. She had not come face to face with Hallowell yet, but she'd heard stories. He was a stickler for accuracy and was known to publicly chew out employees who made mistakes.

"I'm sorry, sir, she's in the library. If you'd like to hold a moment, I'll go get her."

"Please do."

She walked quickly down the aisle and turned into the hallway by the photographers' desks.

Ken nodded soberly at her as she passed.

"Hi." Wynne flashed him a weak smile but had no time to stop and chat.

"Julie, Mr. Hallowell's on the phone. He wants you pronto," she called to Julie from the library's doorway.

"Oh, great." Julie scowled as she slid a file drawer shut and hurried out into the newsroom. Wynne followed more slowly.

When she came even with Ken's desk, she darted a glance around the room. No one was within ten feet of them, and Chuck was still away from his desk.

"What happened to your picture?" she hissed.

Ken shrugged innocently. "What picture? If I had a picture, Chuck would have it on the front page. But I didn't get a picture of that little girl. Too bad."

Wynne stared at him. "You can't just lie like that," she whispered.

"I can't?" He cocked his head a little to one side. "Would you want to see a screaming Hallee Cook on page one?"

She ground her teeth together and looked away. Hallee's terrified face and piercing wails were vivid in her memory.

"Look, Chuck's a little abrasive, but he knows what sells," Ken said more gently. "Just write it up straight, make it as complete as you can without making the family look bad. It will be all right."

Wynne sighed, walked back to her desk, and sat down. Julie was saying into her telephone, "No, sir, I don't think that ran yet. Well, you're right, it should have, but there was that fire last night, and we had to yank something, so we didn't have space . . ."

Wynne was glad she wasn't the one who had to explain glitches to the boss's boss.

The elevator doors clicked open down the hallway, and she hoped it was Karen coming back. She reread the paragraph she had been composing, but inspiration had fled.

"Excuse me, miss."

A man in his seventies was standing beside Wynne's desk. He wore wire-rimmed glasses, and what hair remained made a white fringe around the sides and back of his head. "I'm sorry to bother you. There was no one—" He gestured vaguely toward Karen's desk.

Wynne smiled, although she didn't feel like smiling. "Our receptionist is out for the moment. May I help you?"

"Well, perhaps." He held out a sheet of paper. "This is a notice about a special meeting our church is having, and I told the pastor I'd bring it in today, since I was coming to town anyway."

Wynne glanced around toward Andrea's empty chair. "Well, the person who does the religion page seems to be out as well. Why don't I just take it?"

"Well, thank you." His warm smile lit his face, and his eyes twinkled. "Do you think this could run before Friday?"

"That shouldn't be a problem," Wynne replied. "The religion page comes out on Thursday."

"Oh, good. The meeting is Friday, and the pastor wanted to be sure it ran before that."

She quickly scanned the paper, making sure the date, time, and location were included. The church was a small one in North Belgrade. Every time she drove from Waterville to her sister's house, she passed it, but she'd never been inside. Her family had always attended a different church in the village, several miles to the south. "Looks good. Could I take your phone number, sir, in case we need to contact you for more information?"

He gave it to her, and she wrote it on the edge of the notice.

"We'll take care of it." Wynne tried to sound efficient. "I've never been to Faith Community Church, but I know where it is."

"Oh? You should come."

"Well, I don't live out there. I live in Fairfield Center now, so it would be a little drive." Her rental was about twenty miles from Rob and Rebecca's home, and their church was even farther. In the weeks since she'd moved, she usually went the distance and attended with them and then ate dinner at their house. She enjoyed spending Sunday afternoons with them on the lake.

"It's on what they call the Station Road," the man said. "It was supposed to be the Depot Road, you know. That's what it was called for a hundred years. But when those bureaucrats in Augusta had the sign made up, they made it say Station Road instead. And did the Belgrade board of selectmen send it back and demand a new sign?"

"I'm guessing not." Wynne smothered a laugh.

"They did not. So now we have the Station Road, not the Depot Road. As if it's easier to change it on all the maps than on the sign."

She couldn't hold the chuckle back then, and it felt good to let go of the tension that had been building inside her.

"Well, it's been a long time now, so there's no use me fretting about it," he went on. "See, the church is the old railroad station."

"Really? That's interesting." She and Ken had passed the building that morning, she realized, on their ill-fated safari to cover the tractor mishap. She'd been too nervous to pay much attention, though.

"When I was just a kid," the man said, "the railroad quit using the depot down near the lake, and the church was just starting. They bought the building and had it moved up the road. We've got pictures."

"They must be something."

24

"They are. It made a nice little church."

"What sort of a pastor do you have?" Wynne asked.

"Oh, we've got a good one. We've just recently been able to start paying him full time. It's a small church, but last month we decided we could up his weekly salary, and he was able to quit working for the lumber company."

Wynne smiled. "That's terrific. But I meant, how's his preaching."

"Oh, he's terrific. You come and visit. If you don't like it, I'll be surprised. If you want good preaching, that is. Now, if you just want to be entertained, don't come to our church."

Wynne smiled. "I think I might try it."

"Good! It's only four miles out of Oakland." He waved a dismissive hand. "But you said you know where it is." His blue eyes glittered. "Can you come to this special meeting Friday night?"

"No, I have to work Friday evening. The school board is meeting with the architect, and I have to cover it."

"Oh, that's too bad. Well, I'm going to look for you Sunday. Eleven o'clock. Of course—" He stopped and eyed her for a moment. "Yes, I think you're a girl who would go to Sunday School. I'll look for you at 9:45."

Wynne laughed. "You're on." She had wished at first that he would complete his business quickly and leave, but now she was enjoying his banter enormously.

"What's your name?" he asked.

"Wynne Harding."

"Win? Short for Winifred?"

"No, it's just Wynne."

"Do you get your name in the paper?"

"Yes, sir. If you read the paper tomorrow, you should find my byline on a story about the new addition they want to build at Waterville Junior High."

"I'll read it," he promised. "Don't forget Sunday School."

"I'll be there."

When he was gone, she typed the notice of the special meeting and filed it for the religion page, then went back to her school story. She wrapped it up at four thirty and carefully routed it so that Esther could retrieve the article and edit it for the next morning's edition.

She started to punch in the hospital number again but knew it would be fruitless. After an agonizing moment, she resorted to the phone book and was almost astonished to find a landline number for a Cook family on the Barton Road. She hit the number keys and waited, pushing back her shoulder-length hair.

"Hello?" a woman said.

"Hello, Mrs. Cook?"

"Yes."

"This is Wynne Harding. I was at the farm this morning, after Hallee was injured. I wondered how she's doing. Of course, the hospital won't tell us anything."

"Andrew called me a few minutes ago. They're doing some tests. My husband and I plan to go out after supper. They'll keep her at least overnight."

Wynne frowned. "She had a head injury."

"Yes. They say she's in serious condition."

"May I say so in the paper? Without any details?"

"Well . . . I suppose so. If you have to put anything."

"I'm really sorry. I do have to, and I don't want to distress your family."

"Well, just say they admitted her and it's serious, I guess."

"Thank you very much, Mrs. Cook. I'm sorry to bother you, and I will be praying for Hallee."

"God bless you, dear." The old woman hung up.

Wynne tapped her fingers on her desktop, thankful for Mrs. Cook's openness during such a trying day. The family had enough to think about. Andrew Cook's anguished blue eyes were still fresh in her mind, and she felt a pang of compassion for him. *Lord, comfort him,* she prayed silently. *Let him know you're watching over his little girl.*

She reopened the computer file and quickly finished the story, stating that the girl's head injury had placed her in the hospital in serious condition. She routed the story and checked the time. It was nearly five o'clock, and she began tidying her desk. Her cell phone rang, and she rummaged for it in her purse.

"Hey, Bec," she said to her sister.

"Hi! Just wondering if you're done for the day?"

"Yeah, I'm just about to leave the office."

"Come here for supper?" Rebecca asked.

"Well . . ." She'd be tired by the time she went home, and she had to get up early the next day.

"I'm making fried chicken."

Wynne smiled. "Okay, I'll come. But I can't stay late."

"That's fine. See you soon."

Wynne pocketed the phone and stood, reaching for her purse.

"Good night," Esther said without looking up. "Your school story looks fine."

"Thanks." Wynne headed for the cloak room for her jacket. "Good-night, Julie. 'Night, Karen."

She didn't go to her rental house, but drove through Oakland toward Belgrade. Yes, she was tired, but going to Rebecca's would allow her to escape the hollow emptiness of her rental for a few more hours.

Nearly a year ago, she'd graduated from

28

college and found a part time job at a small weekly newspaper in New Hampshire, where she could live with her parents. But she'd wanted something full time, and since her mom and dad planned to move back to Maine when her father retired, she'd applied for work in the Pine Tree State.

A lot of local newspapers were tightening their budgets and downsizing their staffs, but the *Guardian* had an opening. Wynne was thrilled when she was hired. Early in April, she'd found herself packing for the move.

She'd spent her first week back in Maine with her sister and brother-in-law, but had looked for an apartment or rental house to show her independence and give the couple, who'd only been married a few months, some privacy.

I ought to get a roommate, she thought. The rent was not unmanageable on her salary, and she generally liked her solitude, but she was finding her new life lonely. She had an extra bedroom she could offer.

Now she wasn't so elated. The job at the daily was much more stressful than what she'd done in New Hampshire.

Her spirits lifted as she passed the little railroad depot-turned-church. Maybe she'd make some new friends there. By the time she drove down the gravel road to Rebecca and Rob's house, her usual optimism had returned. She determined not to spend the evening grousing about her job.

Rebecca was a registered nurse, but she'd lost her job in Portland before she and Rob were married. She'd moved back to Belgrade and considered finding a new position, but Rob had assured her she didn't need to. Rebecca seemed happy to set her own hours as she tried her hand at writing fiction. So far she was still unpublished, but they all had high expectations for her.

Determined not to whine to her sister about her own career woes, Wynne tried not to outright complain. She did tell her sister about that morning's trip to the farm.

"I just felt horrid about it all day."

"Oh, poor you." Rebecca gave her a bear hug.

"Thanks. But that's the last I'm going to say about it. It's over with."

They ate supper on the screened porch overlooking the lake. The evening breeze was a little chilly, but Wynne reveled in being so close to the water and hearing the loons call to each other with eerie, echoing laughs.

Rob told them about the project he was working on. As an architect, he helped plan some interesting buildings.

Wynne frowned at him. "I wish you were the architect on that school project."

"Well, no offense," Rob replied, "but I think

the new community center in Winslow will be more fun."

After supper, they played a game, but at eight, Wynne smothered a yawn. "I'd better get home and get some sleep."

"You could stay here tonight," Rebecca said.

"No, then I'd have to get up even earlier and go home to change." Wynne stood. "Sorry, guys. Oh, and I meant to tell you, I'm visiting a different church this Sunday."

"Why?" Rebecca's face showed her dismay.

"A sweet old man brought in a brief for the paper, and we got talking. I told him I'd visit."

"Okay."

Rebecca walked her to her car, and Wynne told her where the church was and about the special meeting she couldn't attend.

"Well, let us know how you like it," Rebecca said.

Wynne embraced her once more and headed out for Fairfield Center. A half hour later, she stopped at the end of her gravel driveway and opened the mailbox. Two bills were lurking there. She carried them into the kitchen and tossed them on the table.

The sofa that had come with the house was brown and had a musty smell on rainy days. She hoped that as summer approached, with its proliferation of yard sales, she would be able to find some bargains on furniture.

For now, a foam pad on the floor had to do for a bed. Wynne's mother had promised her a single bed the next time she went home, and her father gallantly promised that, if she couldn't fit the components into her car, he'd borrow a truck and drive it up for her. But she hoped she could find something locally.

The living room was stark, with just her portable TV on a rickety end table, the musty couch, and the rocking chair she had brought from New Hampshire tied to the top of her car. She had splurged on an inexpensive kitchen table and four chairs, but she still needed a dresser and a hundred other things. She should have left several boxes of books behind and brought more furniture. The books were still in the boxes, waiting for shelves.

A humming from the basement told her the furnace was starting again, and she imagined dollar signs going around on a meter. It was early May, and she hoped it would be warmer soon, but so far the nights were chilly.

She leaned her head back and closed her eyes. Snips of conversation from her hectic workday ran through her mind. Recalling Chuck's derision brought back the humiliation she had felt earlier, and Ken's skewed moral philosophy made her feel naïve and a little bit sad.

The ethics class she'd taken her junior year of college hadn't prepared her for all this—the feelings of incompetence and inadequacy. She wasn't used to being viewed as an antagonist, but Andrew Cook had seen her that way, no question. She admired Ken for wanting to protect the Cooks, and even applauded him mentally for daring to defy Chuck, but the way he had lied so easily to bring about the desired outcome appalled her.

She got her Bible from the nightstand and curled up on the couch with it, wrapping up in the quilt her mother had made for her when she graduated from high school. Its yellow, azure, and white blocks were cheerfully bright, and it smelled a little bit like home.

Andrew sat holding Hallee's hand in the small emergency exam room. His instinct was to pace the tiny space available, but every time he stirred, Hallee began to moan fitfully, so he tried to be still. His mind raced out of control.

The wait for an x-ray had seemed interminable, but now it was over, and he was waiting for the doctor to come and give his report. Hallee was tiny in the white-sheeted bed. Her grotesquely swollen left eyelid made him cringe every time he looked at her. He thought of the close-up photo the *Guardian* photographer had snapped, and anger surged up inside him. The reporter had been young, probably too green to realize how painful this was for the family, but the photographer should have known better.

He tried not to think about the young woman from the paper. She'd looked like a nice girl, dressed conservatively, and a bit nervous. She'd gone a little pale herself when she saw Hallee's injury, but she'd kept a determined set to her jaw. No doubt she had wangled a story out of Grandma and would twist it into a lurid account for the paper.

He stroked Hallee's fingers, and she wriggled a little but didn't open her eyes. He'd tried to protect her and Andy, but he hadn't done so well this time. The E.R. doctor had already mentioned the possibility of an interview with a social worker. He took a shaky breath and began to pray silently, desperately.

Chapter 3

"Wynne, get the police log this morning." Chuck kept walking down the aisle between the desks, tossing off assignments as he went. "Deedee, you're going to interview that poet at Colby College, right? Well, see if you can squeeze in a chat with the developer on the new shopping center afterward. They're talking about modifying the design. Esther, did you touch base with Rabbi Hooper?"

Wynne stood and followed him hesitantly, arriving at Chuck's desk just as he settled in his chair and nestled his coffee mug between his keyboard and a pile of unopened mail.

"Excuse me."

He glanced up, reaching for a letter opener. "What is it, Harding?"

"You want me to get the police log?"

"Right. Dowdy's at the courthouse. Won't have time today."

Wynne swallowed. "All right. I guess."

Chuck frowned, but she wasn't sure if he was unhappy with her or the mail he was scanning. "What's the matter? Jim showed you what to do, right?"

"Well, yes. That is, he took me to the police station the day I rode with him, and I saw him get it."

"So? Is there a problem?"

She gritted her teeth. Jim hadn't been exactly forthcoming on how to go about the task. He'd spent most of the time there gossiping with the desk sergeant, which he'd assured Wynne was a good way to get leads. "No. No problem."

"Good. Do that first." Chuck swiveled slightly away from her, and she knew the conversation was over.

She drove to the police station and entered warily. A window in the wall made her think of a bank teller's booth.

Peering through the small opening, she saw two women with headphones sitting behind a desk, watching the consoles in front of them.

One of them looked up at her. "May I help you?" The voice came from a speaker just above Wynne's head.

"I'm here for the paper. To get the police log. Wynne Harding." She pushed her hair back, wishing she could get rid of the nerves that made her hand tremble as she held her notebook in front of her. A pen and a notebook were as good as a press card in this small city, she had learned.

One of the women smiled at her. "Oh, right. You were here before with Jim. Come to the door, and I'll sign you in."

Wynne scurried the few steps to the door. A city map was mounted on the wall of the bleak hallway, near the dispatchers' window, and there

36

were three doors farther down the corridor. All were closed, and small keypads like calculators hung beside them. She waited by the nearest one, and in a moment the dark-haired dispatcher opened it and beckoned her inside.

"Come on into the com room. We're really busy, but I'll get you started."

She led the way into the crowded room where the dispatchers worked. Wynne sat down on an oak chair that had to be an antique and focused on the logbook the woman placed before her.

Though she tried to screen out the noise of the bustling police station, she could hear footsteps, men talking in the adjacent rooms, and the constant noise of the humming, beeping equipment around her. The dispatchers calmly answered one call after another with barely a breath in between.

With relief, Wynne spotted Jim Dowdy's initials in the margin of the log, where he'd left off on his last visit. She began to scribble frantically. There were dozens of entries to sort through and copy.

A half hour later, she glanced over her work and sighed. Deep inside her was a continuous fear that she would make a foolish mistake with far-reaching consequences. These were people's lives she was dealing with. If she inadvertently transposed a number or misread a name, how much trouble would she cause?

As she left the building, two uniformed officers were taking a handcuffed man from the back seat of a patrol car. The prisoner stumbled on the walkway and cursed. One of the officers grabbed his arm to steady him, and the man jerked away. The second officer seized his other arm.

"Take it easy, Roy. Don't make this any harder than it is."

Wynne shrank away from them as they passed her to get the man inside. Wasn't there another door where they usually took prisoners in and out, so they didn't mix with the public?

She got in her car and sat for a moment to calm her breathing. When her heart rate slowed, she drove back to the paper.

As soon as she entered the newsroom, Chuck looked her way. "Ah, Harding. You just came back from the police station?"

"That's right."

"Turn around and go back."

Wynne stopped in her tracks.

"They've arrested a man who allegedly broke into a house on Mayflower Drive while the owners were on vacation," Chuck said. "He spent the last week there living it up and destroying their property." He smiled at her as though he was handing her a gift.

Wynne pulled in a deep breath, turned around, and headed for the elevator. Was that the man she'd seen them wrestle inside the station? It seemed likely. She would probably have to wait in the lobby for some time before speaking to the arresting officer. She hoped she wouldn't have to see the prisoner again.

On Sunday morning, Wynne drove slowly toward the little church in North Belgrade. Now and then she glimpsed nine-mile-long Messalonskee Lake to her left as she drove south.

Four miles from the center of Oakland, she spotted the building. Its white flank paralleled the main road, and the driveway connected to the side road on her left. Sure enough, the offending sign read "Station Road." Wynne turned, then rolled her red hatchback into the gravel lot before the little church. A dozen pickup trucks and minivans vied for space in the yard.

She checked her watch. Sunday school had already started. Gathering her purse and Bible from the passenger seat, she stepped out into the cool morning. Clouds rushed past the sun, but its intermittent beams shone on a large oak tree at the edge of the lot, revealing a hint of green fringe at the tips of its branches.

Inside the entry, Wynne paused to let her eyes adjust. She was used to churches with light, high-ceilinged interiors, but she reminded herself that this building had been constructed for a less lofty purpose. She stepped into the auditorium.

No tall, stained glass windows or graceful

arches here. The squat little depot had three windows on each side, with deep red drapes flanking them. At the far end of the room stood a platform ten feet square. Red curtains hung from a railing around its edge, and a white-painted pulpit stood at the center front. On either side of the platform was a closed white door, and beyond the front row of folding chairs, an upright piano stood between the edge of the platform and the right wall.

Many of the chairs were empty, and Wynne slipped into a seat in the next to the last row. Several rows ahead, she thought she saw the bald head of the man who had brought her the news item. A white-haired woman sat beside him.

She listened carefully to the lesson, presented by a serious, bearded man in his forties. He smiled occasionally and good-naturedly encouraged the class to take part in discussion. Wynne wasn't sure whether he was the pastor, but he seemed to know his material and had some fresh insights into the Scripture passage.

When the class ended, an older man approached her and held out his hand.

"Welcome. I'm Pastor Fortier." He had warm brown eyes and brown hair graying at his temples.

"I'm Wynne Harding. I enjoyed the Sunday school class."

The pastor smiled. "That was Ray Harder, one

of our deacons. Do you live around here?"

"Fairfield Center. I used to live in Belgrade, but my family moved to New Hampshire. I just moved back into the area. My sister lives on the lake, and I've been attending our family's old church in the village, but I was invited to visit here."

"We're glad you came. What's your sister's name?"

"Rebecca Wallace."

"Any relation to Stewart Wallace?"

Wynne smiled. "Yes, she's married to his son."

"Sure. That's Rob, right?"

She nodded.

"I've known Stewart quite a while. Well, if I can help you in any way, please let me know."

The pastor left her, and Wynne opened her purse to get out the money she had set aside for the offering.

"You came!"

She looked up into the sparkling blue eyes of the man from the newspaper office.

"Hello. Glad to see you." She held out her hand with a smile. "How did the special meeting go?"

"Very well. We had several visitors."

"That's great."

"I read your story about the school, and quite a few since then." His smile told her he approved of her writing.

"Yes, it was a busy week."

41

"How many stories do you write a day?" he asked.

"They expect about three, but I'm not up to speed yet. If I churn out two full-length articles in a day, I'm doing well."

"I saw that one about the burglar."

She winced. "That wasn't my favorite."

"Well, you did a good job. Did you have any trouble finding us?"

"Not at all. I just looked for a railroad station with a steeple."

He laughed. "After church, I'll give you the nickel tour."

Children were coming into the auditorium through the door to the left of the platform, and a few more people came in the front door. The pastor took his place behind the pulpit, and the man left Wynne and returned to his seat. Two children were sitting beside the white-haired woman now, their backs to Wynne.

The old piano had a mellow tone, though it did need refinishing, and Wynne enjoyed singing the familiar hymns. She sang softly, her alto blending with the voices around her. When Ray Harder and another man came down the center aisle for the offering, she held her bills out for the plate, glancing up into the face of the second usher.

She nearly froze with the money in her hand. Hallee Cook's father was staring down at her, his face unreadable. She released her offering and lowered her eyes. He moved on, and she exhaled slowly.

Keeping her mind on the sermon was a challenge. Coming face to face with Andrew Cook again, after seeing him so angry on Monday, was embarrassing. Before she had recognized him, she had been feeling that this cozy little church might be a nice one to attend regularly. But could she come back here knowing it was the Cook family's home church?

By the end of the service, she was calm. Her wilting spirit had been watered. She had the courage now to face another week in the office, and wherever else God sent her.

When the benediction ended, she picked up her green jacket.

"I'd like you to meet my wife." The elderly gentleman led his companion to Wynne's row as she put on her windbreaker.

"Oh, but we've met." The white-haired woman's hazel eyes crinkled as she extended her hand to Wynne. "You're the reporter who was so kind when Hallee had her accident."

"Mrs. Cook!" Wynne shook her hand. "I didn't realize—" She looked at her champion in confusion. "Then, you're Mr. Cook."

"Yes, I'm Thomas. Sorry. Guess I never introduced myself."

"Thomas was in town the day you were at the house," Mrs. Cook said.

"Yes, he came to the office." Wynne's brain was rapidly synthesizing the two encounters she'd had that day with the men of the Cook family.

Thomas nodded, smiling. "Now, isn't that something? Irene told me the reporter who came said she'd pray for Hallee, but I never thought it was you. You were at the newspaper when I went in there, and your name wasn't on the story."

"It was so short," Wynne said feebly, glad Chuck had accepted her brief.

"Well, thank you for not using a picture," Irene said. "Andrew was quite upset that day."

"Then you're Andrew's parents." Wynne turned to Thomas, still sorting the family out in her mind.

"Grandparents," Thomas replied. "And we're blessed with two great-grandchildren in our home."

"Is Hallee all right?" Wynne asked. "I called the hospital Wednesday, and they said she'd been released."

"She fractured her skull." Irene's brow furrowed with concern. "They say she'll be okay, but she needs some monitoring and more tests. There she is."

She pointed toward where they had been sitting, and Wynne saw Andrew bending over the little girl, fastening the chin strap of a purple padded batter's helmet.

"She's got a shiner any pugilist would envy,"

Thomas said with a grin. "Has to wear the helmet every time she goes outside for the next six weeks."

"And no more climbing for a while," Irene added. "They'll x-ray her again later to make sure everything's healing right."

"I'm glad she's okay," Wynne said.

Thomas cocked his head to one side. "You want to see the rest of the building?"

"I'd love to."

Irene smiled. "You go on. I'll wait here and save myself going up and down those steps."

Thomas took her first through the door to the left of the platform, where stairs went down to the basement.

"We used to have a Sunday school room where this stairwell is." He led her down into the cool cellar. "When we put the church on the foundation, they built the stairway."

In the basement there were three classrooms, two restrooms, and a kitchen.

"We don't have a lot of space, but so far it's adequate."

Back upstairs, he took her to the other side of the platform. "This is really the only part left that looks like a depot." He opened the door and led her into a small square room. It was set up as a classroom with a folding table and chairs, but on the right side a deep bay window jutted out.

"This was the ticket window," Thomas said proudly.

Wynne ran her hand over the gleaming old woodwork. Beneath the windowsill were built-in drawers with brass fittings that shone.

"The first pastor lived in three rooms back here. Then we made the auditorium bigger and put the building on the foundation."

"So where does Mr. Fortier live?"

"He and his wife have a little house up the road."

Wynne followed Thomas back into the auditorium, where the pastor was shaking hands at the door. Irene had sat down in one of the folding chairs, but she stood as they approached her.

"Where's Andrew?" Thomas asked.

"He took the children out to the car."

He's probably avoiding me, Wynne thought.

"Why don't you have lunch with us?" Thomas asked eagerly.

"Oh, no, I couldn't."

"Sure you could," said Irene. "It's chicken pie today."

"It sounds delicious, but really—"

"You sure?" Thomas eyed her keenly.

"Yes, but I appreciate the invitation."

"All right, another time." His weathered face was hopeful. "Do you think you'll come back?"

Wynne hesitated. "I enjoyed the services. The

message was a real blessing. Just what I needed today, actually."

"Wasn't it splendid?" Irene asked, smiling.

"Come back tonight." Thomas was as eager as a child.

"I—I might." She was used to attending church morning and evening, and again for a Bible study in the middle of the week. Since her move, she had grown disillusioned. Her sister's church, where her family had attended when they lived in Belgrade, was quite a drive from her rental house. Often she was too tired in the evening to set out. "Do you meet on Wednesday nights?"

"Oh, yes, at seven," Irene assured her. "Can you get out on Wednesdays?"

"I'd like to. Sometimes I have to work evenings." But not tonight, and this little church was a good ten miles closer for her. She made a decision and faced the Cooks more confidently. "I'll come back tonight."

"Atta girl!" Thomas's delight was obvious.

"Come on," Irene said. "The pastor's waiting to lock up."

All afternoon, Wynne hummed the hymns they had sung that morning. On Saturday, she had been to a building supply store and picked up two dozen bricks and some eight-inch pine boards. She stacked them carefully against the living room wall, trying to create a respectable bookcase. Several times she sent a prayer of thanks heavenward. She felt happier, more optimistic, than she had since starting her new job.

Originally, she'd dreamed of moving back to Maine and living with her sister. That was before Rebecca got married. Then she'd hoped to find a rental within a few miles of Rebecca and Rob's home. She'd had to lower her sights and accept a place more than twenty from them, but still—it was much better than living in a different state, and she found time to visit Rebecca often.

She dragged the boxes of books over and began lifting the volumes out, one by one, placing them carefully on the shelves. She aligned the nonfiction by subject and the fiction by author. Austen, Dickens, Forester, Lewis, Stevenson. It was a comfort just seeing the spines in rows. If she wanted an old friend, they were close at hand now. She could hardly wait for Rebecca to see her handiwork.

Her journalism textbooks and reference books went on a shelf together, in a satisfying array. She lined up the books on writing style and usage, quotations, her well-worn thesaurus and dictionaries. The next shelf was soon filled with Bible references and study books.

Wynne eyed the two remaining boxes. She had run out of shelves.

She went to the kitchen and made a cup of tea and a sandwich, then sat down at the table and wrote a letter to her parents as she ate. Phone calls were great, but some things were better written. She described the little church, from the steeple to the ticket window, and related her meeting with Thomas Cook. She didn't say anything about Hallee or Andrew or the accident, but she clipped out one of her bylined articles and tucked it into the envelope.

Thomas entered the dairy barn to begin the evening milking. He passed through the cool milk room, into the large open area where the cows stood in their stanchions, patiently chewing. The warm barn, smelling of hay, manure and disinfectant, was as much home to Thomas as the farmhouse.

Andrew was raking manure and soiled bedding into the gutter behind the cows. Thomas watched him for a moment before turning back to the milk room to get the portable milking machines ready.

The boy had been steady and reliable since he came home to work on the farm. He'd treated his grandparents with respect, and he was struggling to be a good father to his children. But Thomas knew he wasn't happy, and that grieved him.

When Andrew came in to wash up, Thomas ambled over to him.

"Miss Harding said she'll come back to church tonight."

Andrew grunted and reached for the anti-bacterial soap.

"If she comes again next Sunday, Irene and I will invite her to dinner."

"Do what you want to, Grandpa."

Thomas frowned. "You'll be civil, won't you, son?"

"Got no use for reporters." Andrew bent over the sink.

Thomas sighed and left him to begin the monotonous milking session. The comforting throb of the pump lulled him, and he consciously let go of his concern for Andrew. Better just love him, and let the Lord do the worrying. He whistled softly as he went from cow to cow.

Chapter 4

That evening, Wynne drove again to Station Road and parked her car next to Thomas's. He and Irene greeted her warmly in the small entry.

"Come sit with us, dear," Irene said.

"Well, I—" she glanced apprehensively toward the coat rack, where Andrew was helping Hallee remove her helmet and jacket.

"Oh, come on," said Thomas.

She let them lead her to the third row.

"Sit between us," Irene said, settling down on the cushioned pew. "Did you have a pleasant afternoon?"

"Well, yes. I unpacked a lot of my books, and I wrote to my folks and took a nap."

"There, that's good." Irene smiled and patted her hand.

"I've been thinking a lot about this church." Wynne turned to Thomas. "You said you have pictures of when they moved it?"

"Yes, seventy years ago this summer."

"What would you think about a newspaper article about the church? Has anyone done that?"

"Not in seventy years," he said gleefully.

Irene's eyes lit. "We have a clipping of the story they did back then. You could borrow it if you want."

"Will the editor let you write about it?" Thomas asked.

"Oh, I think so. The anniversary will give it what we call a news hook."

"We'll dig out the old pictures and clipping for you," he promised.

The two children bounced into chairs on the other side of Irene.

"This is Andy and Hallee," Irene said eagerly. "I guess you met them last week."

"Well, I wouldn't say I actually met Hallee." Wynne leaned forward. "Hi, Andy. Hello, Hallee. I'm glad you're feeling better." She tried to ignore the purple splotch that surrounded the little girl's left eye.

"The swelling's down," Irene said. "It still looks awful, but it's a lot better than it was."

"Are you the writer lady?" Andy asked.

"Yes, I am."

He came a step closer and looked her squarely in the eyes. "I can write."

"You can?" Wynne glanced questioningly at his great-grandmother. Irene smiled and nodded a little.

"He's learning."

"That's great. So, do you read, too?"

"Yes."

Wynne suppressed a smile at his gruff answer. "Read any good books lately?"

"*Billy and Blaze.*"

"I love that story. Blaze is so brave!"

Hallee tugged at Wynne's sleeve. "Our cousins have a pony."

"That's exciting! Is he like Blaze?"

"Huh-uh. He's a she. And she's fat, and she nips."

Andrew Cook came up the side aisle and sat down beyond the children, at the end of the row. He was broad-shouldered, taller than she'd remembered. He looked comfortable in his gray corduroy jacket and darker slacks. His shining brown hair had been combed into unwilling submission. Wynne looked away, then looked back quickly, to see if he would acknowledge her.

He nodded soberly, then said quietly, "Sit down, Andy."

The pastor stepped to the platform, and Wynne and all the Cooks turned forward. Why hadn't she seen the similarity between Andrew's direct blue eyes and Thomas's from the beginning? Thomas, however, was jovial, while Andrew seemed deeply troubled. Sitting so close to both of them was unsettling. Andrew made the back of her neck prickle every time she saw him, while Thomas made her feel coddled and relaxed.

The pastor called for testimonies, and Ray Harder stood up. "I want to thank God for giving me the opportunity to teach Sunday school this quarter. I'm sure I've gotten more out of it than the class has, but it's been really helpful to me.

It's given me some material to share with my friend John, at work, too. He asked me something the other day, and I knew where to look in the Bible for the answer."

"That's great, Ray, keep it up," the pastor said.

He called for another hymn, and Wynne thought they made a nice trio, with Irene's sweet soprano on her left and Thomas's bass on her right.

The pastor asked for more testimonies, and Andrew Cook got slowly to his feet and stood there, not speaking.

"Andrew," Pastor Fortier said to encourage him.

"I just want to give thanks that Hallee's getting better. It was touch and go there Monday night. The doctors thought she was having a seizure and . . ." He paused, and Wynne felt the pain radiating from him. "I'm just really glad God answered our prayers the way He did, and I thank you all for praying too." He sat down.

Wynne felt an unexpected rush of empathy for Andrew, a nebulous desire to be able to reassure him and take that hurt look from his eyes. She suddenly wondered about Hallee's mother. What had Irene said on Monday? *These kids are all he's got.* His wife wasn't in the picture.

Little Hallee wiggled past Irene's knees and Wynne's, then slid onto Thomas's lap. Wynne smiled at her, and Hallee smiled back, snuggling contentedly against Thomas's chest.

Her mother must be blond, Wynne mused.

Hallee's hair, and Andy's too, was ash blonde. Widowed, or divorced? She glanced surreptitiously toward the end of the row, but Andrew's appearance gave her no clues. *Maybe she's locked in the attic of the farmhouse, like Mrs. Rochester in* Jane Eyre. *No, Thomas wouldn't be so genial if the family had a sinister secret like that.*

The pastor launched into his sermon, and Wynne corralled her attention, taking out her notebook. She reined in her thoughts every time they strayed toward Andrew's side of the church. A meticulous outline of the message was the result.

As they left the building afterward, she took the pastor's hand. "I really appreciated your teaching today."

"Thank you, Miss Harding. I hope the Lord ministered to you here."

"He has. I'd like to come back."

"You'll be very welcome."

She followed the Cook family down the steps. Thomas and Irene called good night to her. Irene had Hallee by the hand, and Andrew walked toward their car with Andy, without looking toward Wynne.

Thomas paused and said, "You're coming Wednesday?"

"If I don't have to work," Wynne agreed. She started to turn away.

"Andrew," Thomas called, and Andrew swung around to face his grandfather.

"I don't think you've met Miss Harding."

Andrew walked slowly toward them and stopped three feet from Wynne.

"Miss Harding." His voice and his face held no pleasure at the meeting.

"Mr. Cook." She felt herself blushing and hoped the streetlight that lit the church yard wouldn't betray her.

He leveled his gaze at her. "I'm sorry I was angry with you and the photographer on Monday. It wasn't your fault. You do what they tell you to do."

"I—it's all right. It was a bad time for you." She was embarrassed that her actions had upset him at the time, and that he felt he needed to apologize now, before his grandfather.

Andy came to his father's side. Wynne caught the glint of a wedding ring as Andrew put his left hand on his son's head and tousled his hair.

"Let's go home," he told the boy quietly.

"Good night, Wynne," Thomas said. "Irene and I will pray that you have a good day at work tomorrow."

"Thank you."

Andrew and Andy were halfway to the car, and Irene waved as she adjusted Hallee's seat belt.

Wynne started her car and turned thoughtfully toward Fairfield Center.

• • •

"Read it again, Daddy!"

"Not tonight, kiddo. It's late." Andrew pulled his son into his embrace.

"I love you, Daddy." Andy put his arms around his father's neck and hugged him fiercely.

"Same here. Go to sleep." He laid the boy down on his pillow, switched off the light, and went across the hall to Hallee's room. She was already asleep, sprawled on top of the covers, a plush bear cub clenched against her pajama top. Andrew pulled the covers over her, easing her feet away from the edge of the bed.

He gazed at her precious face. Very gently, he touched a fingertip to the source of her fracture, high on the side of her head, and traced it forward to the corner of her eye. Hallee yawned and cuddled deeper into her nest of blankets. Andrew stooped lower to kiss her hair.

He didn't stop when he reached the living room at the foot of the stairs, but went out through the kitchen, into the cool, dark barnyard. He walked across the driveway to the pasture fence and leaned his elbows on the top rail. He sighed heavily, staring out over the sloping pasture and at the myriad stars gleaming above. A three-quarter moon peeped from behind a wispy cloud.

He remembered standing in this very spot with Joyce, in the moonlight. She was always bubbling over with enthusiasm about the things that made her feel happy. If she were here now, no doubt she'd be chattering away about that spectacular moon.

She was his opposite, but she'd made him feel complete. He loved science; she loved literature. He was melancholy; she was vivacious. His lips twisted in a rueful smile. Not that he wouldn't give the world to have her here beside him, but still, it wouldn't have hurt her to realize the value of companionable silence once in a while.

Joyce! The stabbing, ripping pain had eased over time, as he'd been told it would. Now it was mostly a dull, aching sense of loss, but every now and then he felt a desperate desire to lash out at death, frustrated because there was no enemy to strike.

What would life be like if she'd lived? He had a mental picture: himself, Joyce, and the twins, together in a rambling Victorian house. He'd be flying for one of the major airlines. She'd be at home with the kids, tying their shoes and teaching them phonics. And they would all be ecstatically happy.

Or would they? Maybe his fantasy was way off base. If he were flying commercial planes, he'd be away a lot, and Joyce wouldn't like that one bit. Neither would the twins. He'd tucked them in every single night of their lives.

And if he had a job like that, they'd have to live near a metropolitan airport. That would mean leaving Grandpa and Grandma behind, because the folks would never leave the farm. No calves and kittens for Andy and Hallee. No brook. No great-grandparents coddling them. Could they be as happy as they were now? And would they be as safe?

He caught the flicker of a green light far off in the sky, over the lower pasture, and followed its movement. As it angled toward him, a red light showed beside it, and before long he could hear the droning engine of a small plane.

He wished he was up there right now, in the cockpit, where his thoughts would be occupied with flying. For a while, he could put aside the Jersey cows and the somber little children who didn't know the touch of a mother's hand.

Seeing Andy talk to Wynne Harding, a total stranger, soberly, as if he were an adult, had caught at his heart. The boy was growing up to be as serious as he was himself. If Joyce were here, Andy would laugh more. Grandma wouldn't wear herself out doing laundry and cooking for them all. Hallee wouldn't be such a tomboy, and he wouldn't ache all over like this.

He knew it wasn't Wynne's fault, but somehow seeing her with the children tonight had brought on this new onslaught of grief. It was a reminder of the gaping hole in his life, in all their lives.

She wasn't a bit like Joyce, but that didn't seem to matter. Her nervousness around him had triggered feelings he'd forgotten. Initial regret for making her feel bad, but more than that. A wish for her approval, and a vague yen to make her laugh. She'd looked happy when she was talking to Grandpa. Pretty and animated, as she'd laughed at one of his silly jokes. But that had turned to definite anxiety when she'd noticed him watching.

The kitchen door opened, and a beam of light shot across the driveway. His grandfather came slowly down the steps and walked toward him. Andrew turned so his back was to the fence and leaned against it.

"Nice night. Not too cold." Thomas took a leaning spot beside him and looked up at the stars.

Andrew said nothing. The little plane was flying northeast, toward Waterville, and was almost out of sight.

After a long time, he sensed that Thomas was looking at him.

"You all right, boy?"

A curt reply was on Andrew's lips, but a rush of regret and despair stopped him. He swallowed hard. "A three-inch crack in my baby's skull, Grandpa!"

"I know." Thomas's hand came down firmly on his shoulder. "Give thanks, son."

A laugh that turned to a sob left his throat. "How can I be thankful for this?"

Thomas was silent for a long time.

Finally Andrew turned toward him. "How come you're not saying, *Be thankful it wasn't worse?*"

"Seems kind of trite."

Tears welled up in Andrew's eyes. "I sure do appreciate you, Grandpa. I don't think I could have handled this alone."

Thomas relaxed against the rail. "Funny how those kids bounce around like they're made out of rubber. They do things that would kill me, and they come off without a scratch. Then something happens that doesn't seem too serious, and . . ."

"I thought she bumped her eye."

"The doctors say her eye is fine," Thomas said quickly.

"I know. It's just . . . when it happened, I saw that purple eye and I thought, hey, maybe we ought to take her in and have her checked over. I had no idea . . . I thought I was being a little overcautious, having Gram call the ambulance." He clenched his teeth, remembering the terrifying moment when the neurologist had said smoothly, *There is a fracture to her skull. Other than that . . .*

"Not your fault. The accident, or not knowing how bad it was."

Andrew sighed. "Joyce—" He stopped abruptly. He hadn't meant to voice the thought.

"What about her?"

"I needed her, Grandpa. I still need her. The kids need her. I don't understand it, and I'm having an awfully hard time seeing any logic to it."

Thomas nodded and stood gazing out over the dark field. Andrew located the North Star and the two dippers. Orion was far down on the southern horizon, and would be lost for the summer soon.

Thomas straightened and stretched his arms. "Logic's not all it's cracked up to be."

Chapter 5

Wynne typed rapidly at her computer terminal Tuesday morning. State funding had been approved for the junior high addition, and she was absorbed in the task of demystifying the numbers for the readers. She wished her brother-in-law was the architect for that job. Rob could explain it to her and show her how to make it readable. Maybe she ought to call him.

"Wreck on 95."

"What? Are you talking to me?" Wynne glanced toward Julie, then back at her monitor.

"They just said it on the scanner," Julie replied. "10-55 with p.i."

"What's that?"

"It's a car wreck with personal injury."

"Oh. In Waterville?"

"On the Messalonskee Stream bridge."

"Ouch."

"Yeah." Julie tucked her auburn hair behind her ears and looked uneasily toward Chuck's desk. "You may get it."

"Me? I'm really busy."

"Yeah, but Jim's gone to city hall, and Deedee's setting up the town meeting schedule. Chuck might send you."

"Oh, boy." Wynne shot a glance across the

room. Chuck was on the phone. She plowed on toward the end of the funding article, trying to get her thoughts down coherently. She could come back to it later and revise a little, but she wanted to get all the major points into the computer before—

"Wynne, you're up!" Chuck didn't even leave his chair. "Get moving! I-95 South, mile 123."

She closed the file and stood, reaching blindly for her keys and notebook.

"Let's have a real story this time." He held out a sheet torn from his memo pad.

She took it without saying anything, praying silently. *Lord, teach me how to respond to this—* She caught herself as several derogatory epithets flashed through her mind, and mentally chalked up yet another spiritual failure.

"Jerry, you go," Chuck yelled in the direction of the photographers' area.

"I'll go." Ken stood up, camera bag in hand.

"No, you've got the hundred-year-old lady at eleven," Chuck snapped.

"Jerry can get it."

"No, Jerry never yet got a picture of a centenarian that didn't make her look like she was already dead."

Ken threw Wynne an apologetic glance. She shrugged and headed for the cloak room. Jerry met her at the stairway door.

"Your car or mine?" he asked.

"I don't care."

"Yours, then."

Wynne followed him down to the parking lot and unlocked the doors of her hatchback. Jerry clambered into the passenger seat.

"I may never get out of this sardine can."

Then why didn't you volunteer to drive your car? She stifled the response and instead asked, "Is the quickest way out Kennedy Drive?"

"No, go to the Upper Main exit and get on there."

"That's right. Southbound." Wynne had only been driving a couple of years when her family left the area and moved to New Hampshire. Her orientation was coming back slowly, but there'd been a lot of changes too. She maneuvered through traffic to Upper Main Street, then to the interstate ramp. A uniformed officer was waving motorists on by. "What do I do? They're not letting us on 95."

Jerry swore. "We're too late. Drive down by Thayer. We can get under the bridge down there."

"You're kidding."

"No, I've got to get a picture, or Chuck will kill me."

She followed his directions to a back road that passed close to the stream. Near the bridge, Jerry told her to stop and jumped out with his camera bag. "Wait here!"

Wynne threw her door open and stood up,

65

screaming at him over the top of the car, "How am I supposed to get my story?"

He didn't look back but climbed a steep embankment toward the highway above.

All right, Lord, you're going to have to help me get this assignment done.

Five minutes later, she stood gasping on the steep hillside, clinging to the top of the guardrail. The wreck had stopped traffic, and several cars were parked on the bridge. Two ambulances and at least four squad cars sat immobile at the far end, lights flashing. Uniformed men swarmed the area near the guardrail. She couldn't see Jerry.

Glad she wore pants to work that day, Wynne climbed over the guardrail, clutching her notebook and pen in one hand. She walked out onto the bridge, toward the scene of the accident, making herself breathe deeply and evenly, not wanting to appear disheveled.

As she drew nearer, she saw that the vehicles involved in the crash were not actually on the bridge. A blue car had plunged down the slope north of the span, coming to rest on its side among bushes and young hardwoods, just yards from the stream. She'd probably been closer to the action before climbing the embankment. A red pickup hung askew above, halfway through the guardrail, the front wheels over the edge of the embankment.

Wynne walked carefully along the edge of the

bridge, past empty cars, toward a tall man in a suit who stood with his back to her, watching the rescue operation below. The wind was quite strong in the middle of the span, and she tried not to look at the water swirling far below.

"Excuse me, sir."

He jumped a little and turned to look at her. A badge was clipped to his belt. "Where'd you come from? You can't be up here."

"I'm from the *Guardian*."

"I don't care if you're from the *New York Times*, you can't be up here."

"Well, I just need a little information, sir."

"You'll have to wait."

She waited, cringing against the guardrail. Silently, she watched with him as rescue workers cut the roof from the car near the stream and pulled a woman from the driver's seat. A tow truck was brought down from the entrance ramp and hitched to the back of the red pickup. Wynne spotted Jerry, halfway down the embankment, snapping pictures. A fireman yelled at him, waving him back.

Wynne cleared her throat and said nervously, "Sir, could you please tell me whom I should ask about the accident?"

"You still here?" He didn't seem to be helping the rescuers, and she wondered if his assignment was to keep timid reporters like her at bay.

"Yes, sir, and I can't go back to the office with-

67

out a story. See, I'm new at this, and my boss will be really upset if I mess up."

"That's a pity." He walked away, toward the rescue efforts.

Wynne took a deep breath. *Well, Lord, begging didn't help. Now what?*

She walked on along the bridge after the policeman, trying to look authorized.

The man stopped next to another officer, and she recognized the state trooper from the Cooks' farm.

"Officer Workman," she said with relief, then realized she might be sounding a little too pleasant for the scene of a tragedy.

He turned his head toward her. "Well, it's Lois Lane. Big story today."

"If I can get it." Wynne didn't look at the man in the suit, but she felt that he was watching her.

"What, Parker won't give you anything?" Workman asked.

"Not yet, sir. I was hoping you could help me."

Parker made a sound like a snort, and Wynne knew her face was reddening.

"You know who this guy is?" Workman asked.

"Uh . . . Officer Parker?" She asked tenuously.

"He's the Waterville deputy chief. You ought to get to know him. Be nice to him. He can help you a lot."

She turned slowly toward Parker and raised her chin and her eyes.

"I'm sorry I didn't recognize you, sir. I haven't been here long."

"That right?" Parker didn't seem impressed.

"Could I get some information, sir?"

"I don't like reporters."

"Well, I don't like paying the rent, but I have to do it."

He grunted. "Drop by my office in an hour." He ambled off toward the ambulance.

Wynne exhaled and turned her attention back to the trooper. "So you're not investigating this, Officer Workman?"

"No, the Waterville P.D. is. But I can tell you the pickup rear-ended the Toyota just before they got to the bridge, sent it into the guardrail and over the edge."

"How many people involved?"

"Seems to be just the woman in the Toyota. There were two guys in the pickup. They've got the driver over yonder, sitting in a squad car. His buddy's in the ambulance that's pulling out."

"So, the driver's not hurt?"

"Ain't that always the way?" Workman spit over the guard rail, and Wynne tried not to let her disgust show.

"Are they charging the driver?"

"Dunno. Parker will tell you."

"Think he'll really talk to me?"

"He said so. He'll see you. Just don't go around

in half an hour. He said one hour, he meant one hour."

She looked at her wristwatch. Bearding Parker in his den at the police station would force her to cut it close on getting to her interview at the opera house.

"Got it. They'll take the injured to Thayer Unit?"

"Natch."

"Thanks, Officer Workman."

"You sure you're old enough for this job?"

She smiled that time. "Oh, yes."

"Come on, you can't be eighteen," he said playfully.

She wasn't sure whether he was attempting to flirt with her or was just being friendly. He had to be at least thirty-five. He wasn't bad looking, but still. Should she snap back, "I'm nearly twenty-four"?

"I'm a university graduate," she said solemnly.

"English major?"

"Yes. But I did study journalism too." Two classes, but she wasn't going to tell him that.

"Of course." He smiled broadly. "Want a cup of coffee? You've got an hour to kill."

"Well, I'm with a photographer." She looked around hastily and was relieved to see Jerry approaching.

"Have you got what you need?" she called to him.

"Yup. How about you?"

"Not really, but Parker says he'll see me in his office in an hour."

"Woo," said Jerry.

"What does that mean?" she asked tartly.

"Going to see the deputy chief in his office."

"So?"

"Nothing."

"Nothing is right," Workman said. "Parker's okay."

"Let's go, then," said Jerry.

"See ya around, Lois Lane."

Wynne waved and followed Jerry across the bridge.

In the car, she pulled a burdock from the hem of her pantleg and tossed it out the window.

Jerry buckled his seatbelt. "I got some good shots."

"Good, because I don't have much yet."

"Just don't tell Chuck," he advised.

At the office she hastily revised the school funding story.

"You going to lunch?" Julie asked from across the aisle.

"I don't think I have time." She smiled, wincing a little. "Am I whining?"

"Sort of. Want me to bring you a sandwich?"

"That would be great. Turkey." She fished a five-dollar bill out of her wallet and handed it to Julie.

The newsroom was quiet as most of the personnel left for lunch. She finished the article and sent it to Esther's directory, then pulled out her notebook and quickly reviewed her notes from the accident and set up a file.

Julie returned sooner than she had expected.

"Come on down to the break room," she called from the doorway. "I'll eat with you."

Wynne looked at the clock. "Okay, but in fifteen minutes, I've got to be at the police station, in Parker's office, and half an hour later I'm supposed to interview the opera house manager."

She poured herself a cup of coffee and unwrapped her sandwich in the break room. Closing her eyes, she prayed silently, thanking God for her lunch and begging Him to stretch the remaining hours of her workday.

"You stressed out?" Julie was eyeing her warily when she opened her eyes.

"A little. Do you know Parker?"

Julie sipped her apple juice. "Only by sight."

"Well, the trooper said Parker will be straight with me. I hope he's right. Parker said he doesn't like reporters."

"He likes Jim Dowdy." Julie took a bite of her sandwich. "Jim has the police beat, and he and Parker are buddies."

"Great. Too bad Jim was in the mayor's office when the accident happened. If Parker keeps me waiting, I'll be late to my interview."

"I hear his bark is worse than his bite."

"But he does bite?"

Julie laughed.

"I'd better get going." Wynne wrapped the remaining half of her sandwich and shoved it toward Julie. "Can you eat that?"

"No, but Scott will. He'll eat anything."

Chapter 6

"I'm supposed to see Mr. Parker now."

"Your name?"

"Wynne Harding."

"You have an appointment?"

"Yes."

"One moment."

It was a good two minutes before the farthest door opened and a blond woman her mother's age, with dark eyebrows and scarlet nails, came out.

"Miss Harding?"

"Yes." Wynne stepped forward.

"The deputy chief will see you now."

Wynne followed her into a second hallway. The woman stopped before an open door. "Right in there."

Wynne stepped inside, where Parker sat behind a desk that took up half the floor space. He was about forty, thin, with sandy hair. Gray shadows rimmed his eyes behind his glasses. His suit jacket lay on a straight chair in the corner beside a file cabinet. The small room was bare of decorations. He waved her to the one free chair and consulted a clipboard.

"All right, here's the accident report. Melanie Giroux, 37, of Topsham, driving south on 95 in a '99 Toyota Corolla . . ."

Wynne wrote as fast as she could, abbreviating when possible. Even so, she had to ask Parker to repeat some things.

"The boys in the pickup are local. White is from Winslow, and Pelletier from Waterville. We've had them in here before."

"What was the cause of the accident?"

"Not sure yet. Speed was a factor, for sure. Pelletier's always going too fast. He's only 19, and had his license suspended last fall."

"So, he was driving without a license."

"Yes, after suspension."

"He's being charged with that?"

"That and half a dozen other things. No insurance, for one."

"That's a law in Maine?"

"It's a law just about anywhere." Parker frowned at her. "You've got to have proof of insurance in the vehicle all the time."

"Right." She felt stupid for asking such a basic question. "It was his truck, though?"

"Yeah."

"Any other charges?"

"We're getting a tox screen. My man gave him a breath test, and he'd had a few."

"Do you have numbers?"

"Point-one-two."

"And the legal limit is . . . ?"

"Point-zero-eight. You should know that."

Wynne swallowed. "You're right. I recently

moved here from out of state, and I haven't had to report on something like this yet."

"I guess you haven't been stopped for OUI in Maine, either."

"No, sir."

"You been writing the stories about the junior high?" Parker peered at her intently from behind his gold-framed glasses.

"Yes, sir."

He nodded. "I've got a boy at the junior high."

Wynne felt he was making an overture, and she seized it. "How old is he?"

"Thirteen."

"Are you happy that they're going to build the addition?"

"Yes, they've needed it for a long time."

"Is your boy an athlete?" She felt she might be wasting precious minutes, but if Parker could end the interview feeling more friendly toward her, it would be worth it.

"He plays soccer and basketball."

"Did you play when you were in high school?" She thought he had the build.

He smiled a little. "I played for Waterville twenty years ago. We had a good team."

She smiled back. "It must be great to watch your son on the court."

"It is. He's really good. He's going to make varsity next year."

"As a freshman?"

"He's good enough."

She nodded. "Sir, I have an appointment with the manager of the opera house in a few minutes. Could I call you when I get back to the office just to see if you have any updates on this accident?"

"Sure. I'll be here."

She left with her spirits high. The interview at the opera house went well, and she was back in the office by two o'clock, determined to complete both stories by quitting time. She did the accident story first, as it was more time sensitive, and she was able to get a list of the formal charges against Pelletier by phone from Parker.

Chuck and the other editors disappeared at three for their news budget meeting, parceling out stories for the different pages.

"You're on page one," Julie whispered gleefully, when she came out twenty minutes later.

"You're joking."

"No, the accident story. Jerry's got a picture so bloody I'm sure we'll get a dozen letters to the editor protesting it, but Chuck's insisting on running it big."

"That poor woman's family." Wynne had just been told by the hospital spokeswoman that Melanie Giroux was in critical condition.

"I know, but it's Chuck's style. The Blood and Gore School of Journalism."

"His and Jerry's." Immediately, Wynne wished she hadn't made the remark. "Sorry."

"For what? You're right."

"Well, I just shouldn't have said it."

Julie shook her head with a smile. "You're strange." She went to her computer terminal. Wynne began typing her opera house story, laboring over the lede.

At 4:30, she stretched and yawned.

"You got that music story yet?" Esther asked.

"Almost done." Wynne really wasn't satisfied with it, but she felt as if her brain had turned to jelly. As she filed the story, she was aware of a man entering the room and stopping at Karen's desk, but she didn't look up.

Karen called her name a moment later. Wynne went for the final keystroke, hit the wrong button, and collapsed in her chair.

"Wynne, this gentleman has some material for you," Karen said.

She gritted her teeth, wondering if her story still existed, or if she had unintentionally consigned it to oblivion. Slowly she turned toward Karen. Andrew Cook stood beside the receptionist's desk, watching her.

She felt a bit lightheaded as she stood up. Andrew was hard enough to cope with at the little church. He definitely did not belong in the office. As he came toward her, she tried to smile, but her dismay over the story, combined with knowing he disliked her, made it difficult. "Hello, Mr. Cook. Can I help you?"

He held out a manila envelope. "Grandpa asked me to drop this off with you. It's the pictures of the church, and the old article."

"Oh, yes, thank you." Her smile was genuine then. "I think it will make a great story."

"You looked a little green there. Are you all right?"

She winced. "I hit the wrong button, and the computer may have eaten my story."

"I'm sorry."

"Well, somebody will help me find it, if it's still there." She shook her head. "I was in too much of a hurry."

"I won't keep you from it. If you have any questions, just call Grandpa or the pastor."

"I will, thank you."

He turned away, then swung back hesitantly. "I almost forgot, Grandpa and Grammy wanted me to invite you to eat supper with us tomorrow before Bible study."

"Oh, well—what time?"

"Five or so. We usually eat pretty early."

"I don't get out of here until five," Wynne said.

"Well, maybe Sunday noon would be better."

"It might be." She doubted he really wanted her to go. He was probably pressing it for his grandparents' sake. "I'll talk to them tomorrow night, but I don't see how I can make it for supper. Please give them my regrets."

"Will do." He stood for a fraction of a second,

then edged toward the hallway. "Well, I've got to go pick up a hydraulic pump before the store closes."

She was surprised that he bothered to make conversation with her. "Oh, are you having plumbing problems?"

"No, it's a tractor part."

"Oh, right."

"For the loader."

"I see . . ."

He nodded and went out into the hallway. She sank into her chair.

Julie was watching her, hands poised over her keyboard.

"I am such an idiot." Wynne pressed her hands to her cheeks.

"Was he asking you for a date?"

"No, his grandparents were asking me for a date. They're really sweet."

"Oh."

"They're farmers."

"He didn't smell like cows."

"I'll think about that when I know if my story still exists. Can you help me? The screen just went blank."

Julie came to her side and soon restored her article. Wynne filed it carefully for Esther and headed home exhausted.

She would have to explain to Rebecca that she was attending the North Belgrade church again on Sunday. Maybe they could get together Saturday instead. She picked up her mail and groaned when she saw bills from both the electric company and her internet provider.

The milk truck was late making its rounds, and Andrew knew they would be late for the Bible study. Will, their part time helper, stayed to help sterilize the milking equipment, and Andrew sent Thomas in for supper. Irene had the twins fed, scrubbed, and dressed for the midweek service when he finally got back to the house.

"Sit down. I've got your plate."

"I'll eat later, Gram."

"No, don't be stubborn. I've been keeping this warm for you."

He took the ironstone plate from her hands and leaned against the counter. "Take the twins and go on. I'll get a quick shower and come after."

"Not if you insist on eating standing up."

Andrew scowled at her over his food. His grandfather entered the kitchen, dressed casually for the service.

"It goes right to your feet if you eat standing up," Thomas said.

"Very funny."

"Is that why Daddy has big feet?" Hallee asked.

"Nonsense." Irene pulled out a chair at the kitchen table and held it expectantly. "Please. You'll get indigestion."

Andrew doubted it, but he sat.

Andy stood as if frozen, staring at the clock above the table. "It's . . . ten thirty."

Andrew laughed. "No, it's ten minutes to seven."

"Head for the car, hooligans." Thomas took his Bible from the shelf near the back door.

"Hallee, where's your helmet?" Andrew called after them.

Wynne arrived at the church a few minutes early and settled in an aisle seat halfway back. Thomas and Irene Cook and the twins came through the door a few minutes later and filled out her row.

"The milk truck was late tonight," Irene said fretfully. "Andrew had to stay in the barn late. He'll be here in a bit. It's just as well you didn't come to supper, but you'll have dinner with us Sunday." It wasn't a question.

"All right, if—"

Irene waited expectantly. Wynne had been on the verge of saying *if you don't think Andrew will object*. Instead, she said, "If you let me bring something."

Irene smiled. "What would you like to bring?"

"Well, I'm not a great chef, but my mother taught me to make yeast rolls."

"That would be wonderful, dear, if you want to."

"I haven't baked much since I moved up here,"

Wynne admitted. "It doesn't seem worthwhile when you're alone. But I think I'd like to pound some dough."

Irene chuckled. "Take out your frustrations on your bread dough? I used to bake bread whenever Thomas upset me, and I sure would pound it when I kneaded it. Of course, that was before I met the Lord."

Wynne stared at her. "What did he do to make you angry? He seems so easygoing."

"Oh, little things. Like when he taught me to drive the truck. I would get so confused, but there were times when he needed me to do it. He would yell at me, 'No, Irene, not the brake. The clutch! The clutch!'" She shook her head. "I never did master the clutch, but the Lord showed us both how to master our tempers."

Pastor Fortier opened the service with a short Bible study from Psalm 133, and Wynne was newly thankful for the Christian fellowship she had found. Andrew came in during the talk, his damp hair dark, and sat beyond the twins. Wynne tried not to look his way again, annoyed that she wanted to.

When it was time for prayer, they separated into small groups. There were about forty people present, and some went downstairs or to the old depot ticket room to pray. Thomas and Andrew disappeared through the door to the stairway. Andy and Hallee went with the Lunt family.

"Mrs. Lunt's their Sunday school teacher, and she prays with the children," Irene explained. Wynne stayed with Irene, and they were joined by the pianist, Tracy Marks.

"Do you have any special requests tonight, Wynne?" Irene asked.

"Just that I'll be a better testimony at work. Some of the people don't try to get along. Then there are some who are good-hearted, but think the end justifies the means." She thought of Ken lying to protect the Cooks. "It's easy to fall into their way of thinking without realizing it."

"Oh, I know what you mean," Tracy said. "I work for an insurance company, and the other women there have ideas I don't agree with. Sometimes it's hard to stand up against what they all think is right."

Wynne and Tracy prayed for each other's interactions with their co-workers, and the three women went through the list of other requests that had been presented to the congregation. When they were finished, Wynne hugged first Irene, then Tracy, with tears in her eyes.

"Thank you. I feel like I've found a church home here."

"We're your family here." Irene squeezed her hand.

"Thanks. My sister isn't too far away, but I don't get to see her as often as I'd like. And this church . . . well, it just feels right."

"If you start missing your grandma or your mother, you come and see me," Irene said.

Wynne smiled and dashed a tear from her eyelashes as the others came back from their prayer groups.

When she drove away later, it struck her that she had succeeded in avoiding eye contact with Andrew most of the evening. She hoped that on Sunday they would find a way to be civil to each other.

Chapter 7

The twins were in bed, and Irene had settled in the living room with her knitting.

"Piece of pie?" Andrew took the pie tin and a gallon of milk out of the refrigerator.

Thomas opened the cupboard door and took down two glasses. "Don't mind if I do. Supper was a mite thin."

They sat down at the table, and Thomas pulled the sports section from the middle of the newspaper that had sat neglected all day. Andrew picked up the front section.

The picture on the front page, prominent above the fold, nearly turned his stomach. An injured woman's pain was etched on her face as technicians pulled her from her mangled car.

Andrew glanced at the headline. *Topsham woman critically injured.*

"They just don't have a clue what's decent," he muttered.

"Hm?" Thomas glanced up.

Andrew started to hand him the front section but stopped as the byline on the story caught his eye. "Figures."

"What?" Thomas pulled the paper around so he could see it. "Anyone we know?"

"Just the writer." Andrew wasn't hungry anymore. He stood up, pushing his chair back abruptly.

Thomas squinted at the print. "Oh, poor girl."

"Poor family, you mean. Everyone in three counties got to see that woman at her absolute worst."

Thomas looked up at him. "I meant Wynne. She must have had to go and see that accident to write this story."

"Ha! Grandpa, your sympathy is in the wrong corner. Did she look upset to you tonight? She looked perfectly happy to me."

"The accident happened yesterday."

"Yeah, maybe she did her crying then." Andrew scraped his pie crust into the small bucket they used for scraps.

"Son, it's her job. Sometimes I'm sure they ask her to do things that aren't pleasant."

"That picture is not helping anybody. If she tries to tell you it's a public service, she's lying."

Thomas frowned at him. "Wynne didn't take that picture. And her story seems very fair and complete. She obviously spent a lot of time getting the facts. What is it about her that sets you off this way?"

"Reporters are nothing but vultures. They feed on other people's troubles. You know it's true."

"I know no such thing. Son, everybody's got to make a living, and everybody wants to know what's going on in the world. We need people in the news business who aren't biased. I think Wynne is doing a terrific job."

Andrew dropped his plate and fork in the sink with a clatter. The anger he usually kept under control surged up in him.

"You wouldn't have said that twelve years ago."

The expression on Thomas's face was too painful to look at. Andrew stalked out the back door, into the cold night. He didn't really want to get into a discussion with his grandfather.

He walked rapidly across the driveway and hopped over the pasture fence. A stiff breeze was blowing. He should have grabbed his jacket. He strode across the field of new grass and climbed a knoll at the side of the pasture.

The moon was past full now, but there was enough light to show him the spot. This was the place where his father had died, so needlessly. The memory was sharp and clear. He tried to pray but couldn't find the words. Finally, he pulled in a ragged breath and walked slowly back to the house.

Thomas was still at the kitchen table, reading the comics, when Andrew went through the back door. He stood up, folding the paper absently.

"Andrew." His hands stilled, and they stood looking at each other for a moment.

"I'm sorry, Grandpa."

"No, I'm sorry. I had no idea you've been carrying that around so long."

Andrew wiped his hand across his eyes, but he couldn't stop the tears from forming. "It was bad enough we had to see him like that, but for the world to see it. It was—" He shook his head helplessly.

"I know. I was very angry myself. Couldn't believe they printed it. I know, boy."

"You can't know."

Thomas's eyebrows arched. "You think I didn't suffer when my son died? Like that? Those round bales were my idea. It was supposed to be a good thing. Less work loading and stacking. Who'd have thought one would roll off the loader like that and kill him?"

Andrew swallowed hard. "It wasn't your fault, Grandpa."

"Is that right? I felt like taking a sledgehammer to that machinery." Thomas sat down, his face gray. "I couldn't sell that baler fast enough."

Andrew sat down wearily. "I was supposed to be down there helping him. If I'd been where I was supposed to be, maybe I could have stopped it somehow, or at least got help for him quick."

"And maybe you could have got killed, instead of your daddy."

They sat in silence for a long time. Andrew closed his eyes to shut out the picture he would never forget, of his father crushed between the massive bale and the hay wagon, his chest collapsed.

"Grandpa, it's not just Daddy."

"I know. It's your daddy, and it's Joyce, and it's all the hard things you've been left holding for a long time now."

Andrew grimaced. "I'm sorry. I've tried . . ."

Thomas nodded. "Son, it's time you quit trying so hard and let God take over."

Andrew moved his hand, unable to express the futility he felt, unwilling to upset his grandfather more by trying to put it in words.

"You listen to me." Thomas leaned forward. "I know you haven't been happy, but you've been faithful. You've taken care of those kids, and yes, let's admit it, you've taken care of me and your grandmother too. Well, maybe it's time you start taking care of yourself. We're past the midnight feedings and diapers. We're past the time for grieving too. You've got a lot of living left, son."

"I don't know. I'm not much good at making changes. I'm the kind that gets hit over the head by them."

Thomas smiled grimly. "A few nights back, you were telling me your life isn't logical. Well, God's planning doesn't always work inside our little logic box. I don't know why things are the way they are, but I know God hasn't let you down. If you start thinking that way, then you deserve to be hit over the head with some changes."

Dear Mom and Dad, *Wynne wrote on Saturday,* I spent the afternoon at Rebecca's house, and now I've got yeast rolls rising. What? Wynne baking? Shocking, isn't it? I am going to dinner at the Cooks' home tomorrow, and I am providing the rolls.

I am starting to love Mr. and Mrs. Cook. They are wise and jolly and would make a good Mr. and Mrs. Claus. They are in their mid-seventies, and full of memories and fun. Their household also includes their great-grandchildren, Hallee and Andy, four-year-old twins, and their grandson, Andrew (the twins' father).

The twins are sweet and a bit mischievous. I have not seen Andrew much, but he seems a tragic figure. Mrs. Andrew is not in evidence, and I feel sure she met a horrible end, although no one has said as much.

Anyway, they are a farm family, and I expect to see some cows before the day is over. Irene is a darling, and makes me miss Grandma Harding. Thomas knows everything about the town's history, and he has loaned me some old photos and clippings to use in a story about the dear little depot/church where they are members.

At work I am kept very busy with everything from school board meetings to fund-raisers. Yesterday I did a story about the quality of the water in the Kennebec River. Believe me, I relied heavily on experts.

I miss you and look forward to your letters and phone calls. Rebecca found a bed for me at a used furniture shop, and Rob borrowed a friend's pickup and brought it up here, so I am no longer sleeping on the floor.

Lots of love, Wynne

She followed the Cooks home at noon on Sunday, with jitters threatening to capsize her confidence.

Dear Lord, it's Andrew, she prayed. *He makes me nervous when I'm around him. He's so silent and serious, I don't understand him. Please help me not to upset him.* She could stand being uncomfortable herself for a while, as long as she knew she wasn't making someone else feel uneasy.

What bothered her most was the flutter of anticipation she felt when she thought of him. When he'd come into the church that morning, she'd realized she was checking to see if his eyes were as blue as she'd remembered. That wasn't good. He'd made it clear he disliked her.

When they reached the farm, Andrew disappeared immediately. Irene whisked Wynne into the kitchen and loaned her an apron. She sent the twins to change out of their Sunday clothes, unbuttoning the back of Hallee's dress first.

"They can dress themselves?" Wynne asked, as the little ones trooped up the stairs.

"Oh, yes, they're quite good at it. Their outfits clash sometimes, but I can't be running up and down stairs." Irene opened the oven to check on dinner.

A delicious smell wafted out, and Wynne's stomach rumbled. The food smelled so good, she could almost cry thinking about Sunday dinners at home. "What have you got in there? It smells wonderful!"

"It's a ham. I'll put the potatoes and squash on and get the salad ready. Shall I microwave the rolls when it's time?"

Wynne helped Irene set the table for six, and they bustled about the kitchen together. The twins returned, wearing denim overalls and long-sleeved jerseys. Andy pelted out the back door, but Hallee stayed with them and was given the job of putting ice cubes in the glasses.

"Smells good in here," Thomas said from the

dining room doorway. Wynne smiled to see him in overalls and a checked shirt.

Irene was draining water from the pan of potatoes. "I've just got to mash the potatoes. You can go call the boys."

When he reappeared a few minutes later with Andrew and Andy in tow, Wynne quickly removed her apron and took the seat Irene indicated at the dining room table, between Thomas and Hallee. Thomas asked the blessing, and the serving dishes made the rounds while Andrew silently carved the ham.

"Pass your plate, Andy," was the first thing Wynne heard him say, then, "Miss Harding."

She held her plate up promptly for a thick slice of ham. The convenience foods she'd been existing on for a month seemed pretty poor rations compared to this.

"This is delicious, Irene," she said a minute later.

"Thank you, dear. Your rolls are wonderful. Very light."

Thomas winked at Wynne and sang, "She looks like an angel looks, cooks like an angel cooks . . ."

"Oh, hush, you. You'll embarrass her so badly she'll never want to eat here again," Irene scolded.

Wynne laughed. "I don't mind. My own grandfather is a bit of a tease."

Andy frowned. "Grandpa, angels don't cook."

"I guess not," Thomas said. "Well, there was that one time with Gideon."

Wynne couldn't hold back a chortle. "I certainly hope I don't cook like *that*."

"I suppose not." Thomas winked at her.

"Sing some more, Grandpa," Hallee said.

"Not at the table." Irene frowned at Thomas, and he resumed eating, his eyes dancing.

Andrew ate silently. Wynne wondered if he resented her presence.

"Think we'll be able to get on the garden soon?" Thomas asked him.

Andrew shrugged. "It's been pretty dry. I think I might be able to take the disk on it this week."

"Good. We need to get things planted."

"Does your family have a garden?" Irene asked Wynne.

"Yes, we usually have a small one."

"Does your daddy grow lemons?" Andy asked.

"Lemons? No, they don't grow where we live."

"He means melons," Irene corrected gently.

"Yeah, melons." Andy rolled his eyes.

Wynne tried not to smile. "Yes, my father usually has a few melons."

"We try to grow melons," Andy said.

"Sometimes we get a good crop, but if there's an early frost, we don't get any." Thomas helped himself to another of Wynne's rolls.

"Last year we got mushmelons," said Hallee.

Wynne laughed.

"We had a few cantaloupe, but the watermelons didn't make it. We're hoping this is a good melon year." Thomas glanced at Andrew. "Better call tomorrow and see if that oil filter for the tractor is in."

"On my list." Andrew didn't look up.

Wynne wondered if he had always been taciturn, or if he'd only been that way since Mrs. Andrew had died or disappeared or gone mad or . . . *Maybe that's what drove her away—him not talking.* Immediately she felt guilty, certain that wasn't the way things had happened. She prayed silently, *Lord, I know that wasn't kind. Forgive me. And please help Andrew with whatever it is that's bothering him so.*

When the meal was finished, Thomas asked, "Want to see the calves?"

"Definitely," said Wynne, "but first I want to help Irene with the dishes."

"Oh, you go ahead, dear."

"No, I insist." Wynne stood up. "We made a lot of dishes today, and I intend to earn my keep."

She donned the apron again and washed pots and pans while Irene put away the leftover food and loaded the dishwasher.

"You have a very modern kitchen for such an old house," Wynne observed.

"When we bought this place, it had a cast iron sink here with a pitcher pump, and an icebox in the pantry," Irene laughed. "It was quite a few years before we remodeled, but it seems like a long time ago now."

"How many children did you have?"

"Five. Jim, Rachel, Andrew, Martin, and Bill."

"Andrew's father was Andrew too?"

"Yes, Andrew Jackson Cook. He was the one who was supposed to take over the farm, but he died early."

"I'm sorry."

"Well, the Lord knows all about it. Andy had an accident when he was only forty. We didn't understand it then, and we don't understand it now, but we know the Lord is in control. Let me just wipe the table, and I'll show you a picture of our children."

Wynne followed her to the living room a few minutes later, and Irene took her to the mantel over the stone fireplace, where several framed photographs were displayed.

"This is Andrew, and that's Jim and Martin and Bill and Rachel." Irene pointed out each child in an old black-and-white picture. The five were standing in a field of corn that towered over their heads.

"That's a nice family."

"Thank you. I have pictures of them when they were older, of course. Sometime I'll show you our albums."

"I'd like to see them."

"This is a picture of the twins when they were three months old." Irene touched an enameled frame.

"Oh, sweet!"

"And this is young Andrew." She picked up a silver frame and handed it to Wynne.

"He was in the military?" Wynne asked in surprise. A younger Andrew in dress uniform and a buzz cut gazed out at her. He looked confident, even a little cocky. So different from the Andrew she saw now.

"Yes, in the Air Force. The twins were born in Germany."

"I didn't realize."

"He mustered out right after that. He had planned to make a career of it, and maybe fly commercially later on, but things took a turn he didn't expect." She smiled tremulously. "It's a good thing the Lord doesn't let us see too far down the road, don't you think?"

"Grammy!" Hallee ran through the kitchen and dining room and into the living room, wearing the purple helmet. "Grammy, where are you?"

"Right here, child. Don't yell in the house. And the doctor said you're not to run."

"We want Miss Harding to come see the calves."

"All right, you take her. Is Grandpa in the barn?"

"He's waiting outside. I'm supposed to bring you." Hallee held her hand out to Wynne.

"I can hardly wait. Coming, Irene?"

"No, I think I'll sit for a minute. You go along."

Wynne went with Hallee, dropping her apron on a kitchen chair. When they stepped out into the yard, she saw Andy and Thomas waiting near a wagon with high, slatted sides. A round steel silo towered high above the peaked roof of the dairy barn behind them.

"We'll go in through the milk room." Thomas opened a door, and warm, moist air hit Wynne as they stepped into a low-ceilinged room with a concrete floor. The smells of milk and disinfectant mingled. Most of the floor space was occupied by a large, stainless steel tank. A motor hummed, and fans whirred. Along one wall were two shining stainless steel sinks, and pipes studded with valves ran along the walls, across the ceiling, and down to the tank.

"We keep the milk in here until the truck comes for it." Thomas opened a cover on the top of the tank, and Wynne peered inside.

"I've never seen so much milk in my life."

"Likely so," he said.

"How many cows do you have?"

"We milk sixty. Then we have young stock."

He pushed open another door, and Wynne stepped into the large, warm barn where cows stood or lay in neat rows between metal pipe

100

dividers, hitched by chains attached to their colorful nylon halters. A constant rustle went on as they chewed and stirred, and now and then a placid moo came, echoed by another animal farther down the row. The permeating odor of their warm bodies, hay, and manure awakened in Wynne a feeling of wholesome, vigorous life.

"It's an old barn," Thomas said. "Most of the stanchions were here when we bought it, and we added some more. Nowadays they use free stall barns, where the cows aren't hitched up. They can wander around and choose the stall they want."

Wynne gazed out over the rows of brown cows that stood chewing calmly, their tails flicking intermittently. She tried to imagine walking into a room with sixty loose cows. "Sounds a bit chaotic."

"Well, it's faster to move them in and out to a milking parlor than it is to milk them in their stanchions like we do. We have to move the milking machines to each cow, and we have a pipeline that takes the milk to the tank in the milk room."

"The calves are over there," Andy cried, sprinting past them toward an enclosure against the wall of the barn.

Wynne walked over with Thomas and Hallee, avoiding the sticky fly paper strips that hung from the ceiling, and peered over the three-foot wall. Three brown calves were curled up together in the pine shavings on the floor. Five others walked stiff-legged about the pen, blatting and snuffling, their eyes wide.

"Oh, they're cute!" Wynne bent over the wall to pat one that stretched its neck toward her. She gasped and drew her hand back quickly when the calf tried to suckle her fingers.

"We help feed them." Hallee climbed up and sat on the wall, swinging her feet.

"How do you do that?"

"With a bottle," said Andy.

"Really? No!"

"Uh-huh," he insisted.

"Grandpa!"

They turned toward the milk room, where Andrew stood in the doorway, his hand on the jamb.

"Uncle Marty's on the phone. Grammy wants you to come."

"All righty." Thomas ambled toward the door. "You'll have to continue the tour for Wynne."

The milk room door closed behind him, and Andrew advanced slowly, as though reluctantly, his hands in the pockets of his jeans.

"We never put a phone in the barn. What else you want to see?"

Wynne shrugged. "I don't know. What else is there?"

"Not much. The equipment shed, maybe."

"I wanna show her the bottles," Andy said.

"Me, too," cried Hallee.

"All right, go get one." The twins raced toward the milk room, jostling each other in their hurry.

"They're adorable."

Andrew didn't say anything but turned toward the calf pen and leaned on the low wall.

"These are Jerseys?" she ventured.

"Yup. They give less milk than Holsteins, but it has a higher butterfat content."

Hallee came tearing back with a huge bottle in her arms, and Andy chased her.

"That is some baby bottle," Wynne said. "I've never seen a bottle that big."

"Lotta things on a farm you've never seen," Andy said.

"That's right," she admitted.

"Flugzeug is butting Houdini!" Hallee pushed the bottle into Andy's arms and scrambled up to sit on the wall again.

"They're just playing." Andrew tugged at one of her braids.

"Flugzeug and Houdini?" Wynne laughed. "You name all your calves?"

Andrew cocked his head to one side. "Well, some of them cry out for names. Houdini got out of the pen the day after she was born. Don't ask me how, but she's definitely an escape artist."

"And Flugzeug? Doesn't that mean airplane?"

He nodded. "That one was a difficult birth.

Grandpa and I had to pull her. We were sweating away when Andy ran into the barn yelling, 'Daddy, Grandpa! There's a flugzeug landing in the pasture!' Didn't know whether to believe him or not, but sure enough, when we got out there, a twin-engine Cessna was parked down at the end of the field. The pilot was heading for Bangor and had some trouble. Thought he'd better land fast."

"So the children speak German? Irene told me they were born in Germany."

"No, no." He stood up and adjusted the hook on the gate to the calves' enclosure. "They were babies when we came back here. I taught them a few words, is all. And the mother cow's name was Liebchen, so it seemed appropriate."

He looked into her eyes for the first time that day, and she felt the disconcerting lurch that had hit her earlier. It wasn't hard to smile at him. He returned her look thoughtfully, not smiling, but not scowling, either.

A door closed, and Wynne was startled to see an unfamiliar young man walking toward them from the milk room.

"Who's that?"

"Will Boyer. We hire him to come in and help us out. Grandpa and I can't handle it all anymore. Grandpa's getting on."

"Just came to get a gallon of milk," Will said to Andrew.

He nodded. "Help yourself. This is Miss Harding, friend of Tom and Irene's."

"How do," said Will.

Wynne smiled. "Nice to meet you."

"I'll be over later." Will turned back to the milk room.

"How long does it take to milk all the cows?" Wynne asked.

"Couple of hours in the morning, and again at night. That's when Will's here. Takes longer without him. Grandpa used to have a full time man, when I was in the service. It's really too much for him, but he insists on being out here in the middle of it. He was about ready to sell the herd five years ago. He probably should have."

"Why did he change his mind?"

"I came back." Andrew pushed the light brown hair off his forehead. "Come on. I'll show you where the plane landed."

He opened a door directly into the barnyard, and they went out, with the twins rushing ahead.

"Warm today," Andrew said, as they crossed the driveway to the pasture. Except for the rail fence on the side that faced the yard, the pasture was bounded by three strands of barbed wire. "The kids like to climb on the fence, so we took down the barbed wire on this side."

Wynne leaned with her forearms on the top rail beside him and looked far down the gently sloping field. Tender shoots of grass were everywhere, and the bright green blanket spread before her for a quarter of a mile, toward a stream hedged by the dark branches of budding alders.

"He landed here?" she asked incredulously.

"Yeah, it's not exactly level, but it's pretty smooth. Guess he thought it was better than putting down in the road."

"You fly, don't you?"

He looked up at the sky and nodded slowly, and she wondered if she had touched on a sensitive topic. "Used to. I try to keep up my hours, but it's expensive when Uncle Sam's not paying for it."

"Do you still have your license?"

"Yeah, but I'm not sure how long . . ." He let it trail off.

They stood in silence for a minute or two, and Wynne wasn't sure where to take the conversation.

Andy and Hallee had run to a wooden swing set. Andy was hanging by his knees from the crossbar that braced one end. Hallee stood below him yelling, "Move over!"

Andrew turned toward them and called, "Hallee, don't you get up there. You're not supposed to be climbing. You can swing, but that's it."

Hallee scowled and stalked to one of the swing boards. Grasping the side ropes, she pulled herself high and plopped into the seat, still frowning.

Andrew sighed. "She's getting tired of the helmet routine. She thought it was cool at first, but she's getting so she hates it now. Her head gets all sweaty."

Wynne smiled. "She'll be a beauty in a few years."

"She's a tomboy now." He shook his head. "Got to do everything her brother does."

"I'm glad she's recovering so well," Wynne said softly. "God was gracious."

He nodded. When he spoke, she could barely hear him, and he didn't look at her. "You're good with the kids. I appreciate that."

The pleasure his words brought was unexpected and intense. She didn't know what to say. He turned back to the view over the field and she asked timidly, "How'd he get the airplane out of the pasture?"

Andrew smiled then, and Wynne's pulse raced. The change in him was astounding, and she couldn't look away from his eager expression. It made her want to listen to him all afternoon, coaxing that smile out again and again.

He leaned on the top rail. "I took my toolbox down, and we tinkered with it. It was all right, just needed a little babying. Then we towed it up to this end, and he got a good run and got off. Just cleared those trees down there, but he made it okay." He nodded, remembering with obvious satisfaction.

Irene opened the back door of the farmhouse. "Cookies and milk!"

Andy bolted from the swing set, and Hallee followed, giving no thought to the ban on running.

"Care for a cookie?" Andrew asked with arched eyebrows.

Wynne smiled. "I think I could eat one. Then I should head for home."

Chapter 8

Wynne didn't have any pressing assignments Monday. She was glad to have a block of time she could use to polish the article on the church. She gave the story and the photo captions to Esther and went to Julie for a lesson in scanning the old photographs. Julie walked her through the process one step at a time for the first picture and then stood at her elbow, coaching her through the second one.

"You're doing great. Looks like something that goes with an interesting story."

"It's a little church celebrating its seventieth anniversary. It was a railroad depot. In this picture, they're moving it on a truck from the railroad tracks to where it is now."

"Neat." Julie removed the photograph from the scanner. "How'd you find it?"

"One of their members brought in a press release a couple of weeks ago and invited me to visit the church. I did, and I loved it. I've decided to attend there regularly. It's a good church."

"How do you know a good church when you see one?"

Wynne was caught off guard and tried to marshal her thoughts quickly. "Well, I always want one where they teach the Bible and believe everything it says."

"Everything?" Julie seemed doubtful.

"Well, yes. I believe everything in the Bible is true."

"Like people walking on water, and demons, and things like that?"

Wynne nodded slowly. "That doesn't mean it's happening nowadays. I don't know what you've heard, but if it's in the Bible, I believe it."

Julie eyed her speculatively. "I tried to read the Bible once, but it was confusing, and I couldn't find anything about the things I really wanted to know."

"What kind of things do you want to know?"

"Well, for one thing, when I do something wrong and I feel guilty about it, I don't know if I can really set it right. With God, I mean. Do I just have to be guilty forever?"

Wynne smiled. "There is a really wonderful verse in the Bible that talks about that. Do you want to eat lunch with me today, and I'll show it to you?"

Julie hesitated only an instant. "Okay. But maybe it will be noisy in the break room."

Wynne wondered if she didn't want any of their coworkers to overhear the discussion. "It's warm today. Let's get sandwiches and go over to the park. We can talk there."

● ● ●

"I had no idea all this stuff was in the Bible. I guess I didn't read far enough." Julie scanned the page Wynne had opened for her.

"There are all sorts of wonderful things in that book."

They sat on a park bench near city hall, eating the last of the corn chips Wynne had brought along. The sun warmed them, and Wynne felt confident at last that Maine would actually have a summer.

Julie took another chip. "These things are awful for you, you know."

"Yeah. I've got a study book at home." Wynne brushed crumbs from her skirt. "It takes you through some really basic teachings in the Bible, and it explains some of the verses. I'll bring it in tomorrow and you can borrow it. If you're interested, it will help you a lot."

"A theology book?"

"No, it's not like that. It's pretty easy reading."

"Well, okay. But if it's boring, I warn you I won't read it."

"Well, it's Lois Lane!"

Julie and Wynne turned toward the state trooper who was coming down the steps of city hall, grinning from ear to ear.

"Hello, Trooper Workman." Wynne couldn't help smiling.

"Who's your friend?"

"Julie Saxton. She's one of my editors."

"Hi there," Workman said in Julie's direction, but his eyes stayed on Wynne's face. "So, lunch in the park."

"Yes, but we need to go back to the office soon." Wynne looked at her watch and tried to telegraph Julie with her eyes to back her up.

"Good write-up on the accident," Workman said. "I guess your chat with Parker went okay."

"Yes, he was very good about it."

"When are we gonna have that cup of coffee?" He lowered his voice to a confidential level, and Wynne saw that Julie was listening avidly.

"Oh, I don't know, Mr. Workman. Not today, I guess. I'm pretty busy."

"It's Dave."

"Well, you know, I've got to do my work." Wynne felt the familiar blush creeping into her cheeks. Her social life wasn't much lately, but she wasn't sure how to gracefully turn down a gregarious cop who spat in the middle of conversations.

"If you had come ten minutes earlier," Julie piped up, "you could have eaten tuna sandwiches and corn chips with us."

Workman looked at her, then back at Wynne. "Can I talk to you?"

"Sure." Wynne didn't move from the bench.

"I mean privately."

"Guess that's my cue." Julie rose with a grin. "I'll see you, Wynne."

"No, wait," Wynne cried, but Julie was striding toward the edge of the park and the street that separated it from the office building, and Dave was sitting beside her on the bench. "I really need to get back," she said feebly. "My lunch hour is over."

"Then just say one word. I ask you a question, and you say, 'yes.' Got it?" Dave leaned toward her, and Wynne edged away uneasily.

"What's the question?"

"Go out with me?"

"No."

He frowned. "That's not your line."

"I'm sorry." Wynne stood up.

"What is it about me that you don't like?"

"I don't know you." She picked up her purse and her Bible.

"I'm trying to get to know you."

She looked him full in the face. "Mr. Work-man—Dave—I have to tell you up front, I don't usually go out with a man unless I know him pretty well and we're on the same wavelength."

"So, how do you get to know a man if you won't spend time with him?"

She sighed. "I just . . . don't think we have the same values, the same priorities."

"What makes you think that?"

"Look, I really am going to be late. Isn't it

easier if I just say I don't want to go out with you?"

"No. I still want to know why."

She began walking toward Front Street. Dave fell into stride with her, and she knew she couldn't avoid a discussion. "For starters, we have a big age difference."

"You said you're over eighteen."

She looked at him out of the corner of her eye, but he seemed to be serious. "I'm twenty-three."

"And I'm thirty-four. So?"

She paused on the sidewalk, waiting for a lull in traffic. "Are you married?"

"No. So that's one in my favor, right?"

"Ever been married?"

"Uh . . . let's come back to that one."

"No, I don't think so."

He was still beside her when she stepped off the curb. "Just like that? You won't even give me a chance?"

She stopped outside the door to the office, afraid he would follow her inside if she didn't. "Dave, I don't have time to get into a philo-sophical discussion right now. If you really care about my reasons for turning you down, I'll tell you sometime, but it will take a few minutes, and I don't want to feel pressured when we talk, okay?"

He smiled slowly. "So, maybe we can get that cup of coffee sometime?"

She met his eager look with resignation. "Only

so I can explain my feelings to you. I'll have coffee with you, but with the understanding that it is not a date, and I don't intend to make a date with you."

"That's fine. I'll drink coffee with you for any reason. What time do you get done here?"

"Five o'clock."

"I'll be here."

He turned and walked across the street toward the police station. Wynne saw his state police cruiser in the municipal parking lot. She watched him for a moment then shook her head and went inside.

Karen pounced the moment she entered. "Julie says you've got a state trooper dangling after you."

Wynne glanced with exasperation toward Julie, who was sorting papers at her desk.

"Sorry." There was no compunction in Julie's voice. "He was giving you this big come-on, and I had to tell somebody. This is the newsroom, after all, and I thought it was big news."

Wynne put her Bible in the desk drawer and took off her sweater.

"So, are you going out with him?" Karen persisted.

"Who is it?" Deedee Rollins asked from the other side of the divider.

"Whoever he is, he's not bad looking," said Esther.

Wynne gasped, realizing that the entire news-room had been discussing her run-in with Dave. "You saw him?"

"Sure." Esther nodded toward the large windows overlooking the street and the park.

"So, who is he?" Deedee repeated.

"His name is Dave Workman." Julie kept on working as she talked.

"I know him," Deedee said eagerly. "He was on that drug raid I covered last week. He's passable."

"I'd go out with him," said Esther, and Wynne stared at her. "If I wasn't married," Esther added.

"He's good looking. Kind of old for Wynne." Julie clipped a sheaf of papers together.

"He's not old," Scott called from the desk below Deedee's. "He's younger than I am."

Wynne decided the best course of action was to ignore them all. She picked up a fax someone had left on her desk during lunch. It was an item she could type up as a news brief, and she opened a new computer file.

The chatter calmed down, and soon everyone was working hard. Wynne wondered if she could possibly keep her coworkers from seeing her meet Dave at five o'clock.

"Wynne."

She looked up to find Chuck standing beside her desk.

"What is it?"

"Take tomorrow off. I need you to cover the graduation at Thomas College Saturday."

"Okay," she said uncertainly. "What do I do?"

"Go to the graduation, listen to the speaker, and write a twelve-inch story for Sunday's paper. Give it some color. Ken will be taking pictures. If you do a good job, I'll have you do the graduation at Colby the next week." Chuck walked away.

"If you're too good, he'll make you go to every high school graduation within twenty miles, too," Deedee said just loudly enough for her to hear.

"Am I being given drudge work?" Wynne looked across the divider at Deedee's too-perfect makeup and blond French braids.

"Major weekend drudge work. Last spring I copped four graduations. But we've got a rookie reporter this year, so maybe I won't have to do any." Deedee smiled sweetly.

Wynne wasn't sure she'd know what to do with herself, having a Tuesday off, but as she worked a plan began to take shape in her mind. As soon as she got home, she would call her sister. At five o'clock she called a cheerful good-night to Julie and headed for the stairway. She could always beat the elevator by taking the stairs.

As she turned the corner in the stairway, she came face to face with Dave Workman.

"There you are! All set?"

Her eyes were on a level with his, although he

was two steps below her. "Oh, Dave. Uh, sure. Where are we going?" She didn't want to insult him by letting him know she had forgotten their agreement.

"How about Steve's?"

"That's a fancy restaurant, isn't it?"

"So, we could get a bite to eat."

"No, Dave. I said coffee."

"Well, it's supper time. Aren't you hungry?"

"Maybe a little, but I really meant it when I said we'll have coffee and talk."

The door above them opened, and he turned to walk down the stairs with her. "All right, you win. How about that gourmet coffee store on Main Street?"

It was an hour before she could get away. Dave began by trying to charm her into changing her mind. When that failed, he agreed to listen to her reasons for refusing a date with him.

"Come off it," he said incredulously after Wynne had tried her best to explain her beliefs without being offensive. "You can't be one of those whacko, bigoted fundamentalists."

Wynne stirred her coffee. "Well, I wouldn't describe myself that way."

"Nah, I don't believe it."

"Why is that so strange? Haven't you ever met a Christian before?"

"Well, sure, I suppose so, but normal people

118

don't go to church more than once a week, and they don't go around spouting quotations from the Bible at each other."

"I'm sorry if I've offended you, Dave, but it's a very important part of my life. I believe that I'm a sinner, and only God can do anything about that."

"Oh, man. Now, that. See, that is where you don't sound credible."

"What do you mean?"

"That's not normal talk. You sound like an ultra-right-wing weirdo."

She sipped her coffee, praying, *Lord, help me not to take offense or give it.*

"Well, I guess you don't really want to date me after all, now, do you?"

"Come on, Lois. Wynne. You're not serious."

"I am."

"But you look so—"

"Normal," she supplied.

"No, that's not it. You look better than normal. I figured you were holding me off because of my age or something, but now it sounds like you want a preacher. Aren't you being a little picky here?"

She sighed. "The Bible says Christians shouldn't marry non-Christians, and I know I wouldn't be happy if I married someone who didn't believe the way I do."

"Hey, who's talking marriage here?" he asked

hastily. "I just wanted to take you to a movie or something."

She shook her head. "It wouldn't work. I'm sorry, because you seem like a nice guy, and I don't want to make you feel bad, but I just can't."

He looked at her thoughtfully. "That's the weirdest reason a girl ever gave me for turning down a date. You're not just making this up—"

"No."

"Well, then, I guess I know where I stand."

She sighed in relief and crumpled her napkin.

"So, you think I'm going to hell?"

She hesitated, wondering if it was possible to answer his question without making him angry or sounding pious. "The Bible teaches that hell is a real place."

His eyes locked to hers. "You really believe all that."

"I do. And I think this is probably the only chance I'll ever get to tell you about what Jesus did for us. He made it possible for everyone to be forgiven and spend eternity with God."

He looked around the room, at the tables and coffee machines and glass jars of jelly beans. "I liked you. I *really* could have liked you."

She reached for her purse. "Can't we stay on friendly terms?"

"Oh, sure. When you come to a wreck I'm investigating, I'll give you all the dope, and

I won't try to sabotage you. But I don't expect you'll stay with the paper long."

"Why not?"

"You're too conservative. The news business chews up people like you and spits them out."

"I guess we'll see about that. Now I should go home."

"Yeah. Sure." They stood up, and he walked with her to the door. "Listen, if you wake up one day and decide you've had enough of that—" He stopped abruptly. "No, I guess you wouldn't. You're too sweet. You really believe it."

Wynne took her car keys out. "Good night, Dave. Thanks for the coffee."

She took a shower and ate a light supper before she regained her eagerness to call Rebecca. She'd had the chance to share her faith with two people that day, and their different reactions replayed over and over in her mind. Julie's skepticism and Dave's outright rejection. Her lingering disappointment was in itself discouraging. Shouldn't she be glad that they had at least heard her out?

She called Rebecca and blurted, "I have tomorrow off unexpectedly. Do you want to do something together?"

"I'd love to, but I can't. Rob wants me to go with him to Madison. They're cutting the ribbon at a medical building he designed last summer."

"Oh, okay. No problem." They chatted for a few more minutes and then hung up. Wynne felt very alone. After a few minutes' thought, she gathered her courage and called the Cooks' house.

"Irene, it's Wynne. I have tomorrow off, and I wondered if you could go shopping with me?"

"Oh, that sounds like so much fun! But the children . . ."

"We could take Andy and Hallee with us. Maybe we can end up at the North Street Park afterward. There's a huge playground there."

"The twins are so antsy," Irene objected. "Not the best shopping companions."

"Well, I really need a dresser. I was hoping to get one at a yard sale, but there haven't been many yet, and now it looks like I might have to work Saturdays for a few weeks, so I thought I'd just bite the bullet and buy a new one."

"Goodness, child, you don't have a bureau?"

"No, I'm living out of boxes and a rather dilapidated suitcase."

"Well, we've got more bureaus than you could shake a stick at. There's an empty one in Rachel's old room, and there's another in the attic—"

"Oh, no, I didn't call for a handout," Wynne protested. "I really was after your company for tomorrow. My sister's tied up, and I wanted a friend I could do something with."

"I'm honored. I'll tell you what. I have to be here to feed the men lunch, but I could spend the morning with you if I plan it right. Thomas and Andrew can look after Andy and Hallee for a few hours. I never seem to get out with another woman anymore."

Wynne's enthusiasm returned. "Let's do it! We can try on hats and find a card for my mother. This Sunday is Mother's Day, and I haven't done a thing about it yet."

"All right, dear, I'll talk to Thomas and call you back. I can start a stew tonight and leave it simmering. Yes, that would work. But you must come back here with me for lunch."

With Will Boyer's help, Thomas and Andrew were out of the barn an hour after Irene left to meet Wynne for the shopping expedition. The mailman drove in and honked his horn, the usual signal for a package, and Andrew walked out to get it.

"Is it a toy?" Hallee asked, scampering in a circle around her father as he juggled the package while sifting through the mail.

"Likely it's cow medicine." Andy's blue eyes were round and serious.

"Both wrong." Andrew opened the kitchen door, and the twins scuttled past him, waiting eagerly as he took the package to the table.

"It's about time." Thomas took out his pocketknife and slit the tape on the box.

"Pumpkins!" Hallee screamed.

"Pumpkin seeds." Thomas lifted out the top seed packet and put it in her hand.

"Got any lemon seeds, Grandpa?" Andy asked.

"Cantaloupe and watermelon." Thomas flipped through the packets. The twins hovered anxiously as their great-grandfather compared the contents of the box with the packing list.

"I want to plant the peas," Hallee shouted when she spotted the packet picturing plump pea pods.

"Hush," Andrew growled.

"When can we plant?" Andy asked.

"Maybe this afternoon. I told your Uncle Pete I'd go over there this morning and look at his planter."

Thomas lifted a package of squash seed and squinted at it. His eyes crinkled behind his glasses. "Blue Hubbard. Did we get any buttercup?"

"Must have forgot. I'll pick some up at Agway."

"Irene's got to have buttercup." Thomas gathered all the packets and put them back in the box. "Pete got trouble with his planter?"

"I think it just needs adjusting."

"Why don't we all ride along?" Thomas closed the flaps of the box. "I haven't talked to Bob for a while, and it might be a good day for certain people to see the p-o-n-y."

"Pony," Hallee shouted.

Thomas laughed, but Andrew scowled at Hallee.

"Getting so's you can't even have a private conversation around here."

"Don't fret," his grandfather said. "You've got the smartest kids in Kennebec County, and that's nothing to complain about."

"Are we going to Grandpa Turner's?" Hallee asked, hanging on Andrew's elbow.

Andrew lifted his arm, straining against her weight. "I might go over there, if I didn't have this monkey on my arm."

Helen Turner came out of the weathered house as Andrew braked in her driveway.

"Andrew! I'm so glad you brought the children over."

"Nana, We want to see Duchess!" Hallee scrambled over Andy when he opened the car door, and into her grandmother's arms.

"Well, now, I'll bet Duchess wants to see you." Helen's smile softened as she watched Andy climb out of the back seat. "Hello, Andy. Do you want to see Duchess too?"

He nodded, and Helen laughed, bending down to kiss him. "Aunt Donna's feeding the calves. She'd probably get Duchess out if you asked real nice." She straightened. "Where's Irene this morning?"

"Gone shopping," Thomas replied.

"Tom's here," Bob Turner called, ambling toward them from the young stock barn. "Must be time for a coffee break."

Thomas laughed. "Well, now, there's a capital suggestion!"

"Andrew?" Helen asked.

He started to speak, but Hallee tugged at his pantleg. "No, no, no. No coffee."

"Be polite." Andrew smiled apologetically at Helen. "I'll just take the kids out to the barn. Hallee, get your helmet out of the car. No pony rides without that."

"You'd never know she was hurt. She's as lively as ever." Helen shook her head, smiling.

"She's all the time boiling over," Thomas agreed.

"Just like Joyce."

Andrew turned to help Hallee with her helmet, avoiding his mother-in-law's eyes. These constant reminders kept him away from the Turners' farm.

He knew Helen didn't mean to make it more painful for him, but it seemed she couldn't see the twins, especially Hallee, without reopening the old wounds. He used his constant work as an excuse for not coming more often. It was only a mile, but over the last four years he had made the trip less and less often.

When he had first brought the twins home, Andrew took them to see Joyce's parents. Helen had fussed over them a bit, but then broke down weeping.

"If only you hadn't taken her so far away," she sobbed. Andrew left feeling he was to blame.

126

During the next few months, Helen had visited once. She wanted to hold Hallee, but she left after just a few minutes, again in tears. The rest of the Turner family visited when their busy schedules allowed. Andrew's sisters-in-law adored the babies and offered to babysit frequently, but he seldom took them up on it.

He knew Bob and Helen loved the twins, but he also knew Helen couldn't forget the way Joyce had died thousands of miles beyond her reach. She always seemed pleased when he brought the children over now, but he wondered if she wasn't relieved when he left.

He took Andy and Hallee's hands firmly in his. Donna Turner waved to them from the calf hutches between the dairy barn and the hay barn. Donna was married to Joyce's brother Henry, and she had been a close friend to Joyce in the old days. Her two-year-old son, Nicky, toddled toward them.

"Hey, there, you want to help me, kids?" Donna called.

Hallee broke away and ran to the pen. Andy stayed with his father, trying to match his stride. Halfway to the hutches, Andrew scooped up Nicky and carried him.

Donna gave Hallee the milk bottle to hold for a little Holstein calf. "You can go in the barn if you want, Andrew. I'll get Duchess out when I'm done here."

"You don't mind?"

"Of course not."

"Think Duchess will be frisky? I don't want to take a chance with Hallee."

"That old thing?" Andy scoffed. "She's slow as a slug."

Donna laughed. "Duchess is pretty calm, but I'll hold on tight. And Hallee's got her helmet. Go ahead, Andrew. We'll be fine." She held out her arms for Nicky.

In the barn, Andrew found Joyce's brothers, Pete, Henry, and Bob Jr. The Turners milked more cows than the Cooks did, to support the large extended family, and the milking lasted nearly four hours, morning and evening.

The brothers greeted Andrew cheerfully. Pete, his best friend since childhood, took him out the back door and into the equipment shed. After fifteen minutes of tinkering, Andrew declared the aging planter to be in working order.

"No one here's got the touch you have, Andrew, my man." Pete slapped him on the shoulder.

"Well, if you'd fix things right, instead of sticking them together with baling twine and bubble gum . . ."

"Hey, watch it! I don't come to your place and insult your equipment."

"That's because my equipment runs."

Pete nodded toward the far side of the shed. "Seen the new chopper yet?"

"Nope." They walked over and inspected the machinery. "Well, you needed it," Andrew conceded.

"You tired of milking cows yet?"

Andrew pressed his lips together. "The truth?"

"Nothing but."

"I been tired of milking for a long time."

Pete opened his mouth as if to speak, then closed it again. Andrew bent down to examine the chopping blades more closely. He knew what was on Pete's mind, and he appreciated Pete's not voicing it.

Pete and Judy and their three children were crowded into the old hired man's house on his father's place, and the main farmhouse was bursting at the seams with the other boys and their families. The Turners had been negotiating to buy the Cooks' farm before Andrew came home, and if he'd stayed away, Pete and Judy would probably be living in his grandparents' house right now.

Pete leaned against a post. "Judy and I are looking at a couple hundred acres in Readfield tomorrow."

"Really?"

"Yeah."

Andrew stood up and made himself meet Pete's eyes. "I'm sorry."

"No need."

"Things didn't go the way you planned. I feel like it's my fault."

Pete shook his head. "None of it's your fault, Andrew. I just hate to see you wearing yourself down to a stub on that farm when you'd rather be someplace else."

Andrew had no answer for that. It was too complicated. But maybe he didn't need one. Pete knew he had to provide for the twins and his grandparents, and how families stuck together when things got rough. And Pete knew about the dreams he had mothballed when he buried Joyce.

"How are your folks taking it?"

Pete grimaced. "They don't want us to move away. But there's not enough ground here to keep us all. We're driving six, eight miles to hay fields we're renting. We're just overextended. I know it will be better for all concerned if we go."

"Pete, I—"

"Don't say it. If I'd been in your position, I'd have done the same thing."

Chapter 9

Wynne and Irene walked down Main Street together, wandering in and out of little shops Wynne hadn't had time to discover. Irene took her into a gift shop, where she bought cards for her mother and grandmother, and sets of stationery with Maine scenes.

"Now for the dresser." Wynne followed Irene's directions to a furniture store, but she decided the prices were beyond her means.

"I'd better get an unfinished one at a department store."

"Don't decide yet, dear."

"Well, I need to do something."

"There's a coffee shop down the street. I think we need a cup of tea. Or coffee. Whatever you like." Irene guided her into the shop and insisted on treating.

Wynne didn't mention that she'd had coffee in the same place the evening before with Dave Workman. With Irene, the atmosphere was changed, and she found her spirits lifting.

"This is the most fun I've had in weeks." Irene's eyes glinted as she nibbled her pastry.

"It's the most fun I've had since I started working for the paper," Wynne admitted.

"Oh, you poor thing. We'll have to make sure

you see more than the new school addition and city hall."

At noon they drove into the Cooks' driveway, and Irene sent Wynne to the barn to find the family while she hastily put lunch on the table.

Wynne opened the door to the milk room cautiously. Thomas and Hallee were inside, and Thomas greeted her with a broad smile.

"Miss Harding!" Hallee ran toward her, Wynne knelt to embrace the little girl.

"Don't you think you could call me Wynne?"

"Daddy says not, because you're a grownup." Hallee's mouth drooped. A strand of damp blonde hair clung to her forehead below the rim of her helmet.

"All right, I wouldn't want to argue with your daddy, but personally, I wouldn't mind." She looked up at Thomas. "What do you think of 'Miss Wynne'?"

Thomas's eyes twinkled. "Might pass muster."

She nodded and turned her attention back to Hallee. "Did you have fun this morning?"

"Yes, we went to Nana Turner's, and we rode the pony."

"The fat one that nips?"

"Mm-hm, but she didn't bite today."

Wynne squeezed her. "I'm glad. Lunch is ready. Where are Andy and your daddy?"

"They're out back, working on some new calf hutches," Thomas said. "Do you want to call

132

them for lunch, and Hallee and I will go wash up?"

Wynne left them outside the milk room and followed the sound of hammering around the corner of the barn. Beyond the silo, Andrew was driving a nail in the flat plywood roof of what looked like a large doghouse. Andy stood beside him, ready to hand him the next nail. Andrew looked up as she approached.

"Miss Harding, have a nice day in the big city?" he asked.

"Yes, thank you," she smiled. "Irene and I had a grand time."

"Spend all your money?"

"No, actually we didn't spend much. Just spending time together was more fun."

He handed the hammer to Andy. "Put that in the toolbox."

The boy stooped to put it away.

"I'm supposed to tell you lunch is ready," Wynne said.

Andrew nodded. "Go get washed, Andy."

The boy sped toward the house, and Andrew picked up the toolbox.

"So, the calves are going to have private rooms now?" Wynne surveyed the three finished hutches and a waiting pile of plywood.

"Yeah, we need to get them outside. I'll just put this in the barn."

Wynne waited while he put the toolbox away.

133

His eyes flared when he came out and saw her, and she flushed a little, thinking she shouldn't have waited for him.

They walked slowly side by side, and she thought she should say something because he wouldn't, and it would be awkward, but suddenly he spoke up.

"I like May. It's a nice time of year. Everything greening up again." He squinted briefly up at the sun.

"I was born in May." Wynne felt a bit shy as she said it.

Andrew smiled and opened the back door to the kitchen for her. "Guess you're just a spring chicken."

She laughed, and Irene looked up from the biscuits she was taking from the microwave when she heard it. She smiled at the two of them. "We're ready to sit down."

"I'll just wash up." Andrew stepped to the sink and rolled up the sleeves of his blue plaid shirt.

"Let me take that in for you." Wynne reached for the basket of biscuits and followed Irene to the dining room. She took the chair she'd had before, between Thomas and Hallee, and when Andrew sat down they all joined hands for the blessing.

"Now, Wynne, after lunch we'll go upstairs and look at those bureaus." Irene ladled stew into

Andy's bowl. "If one of them suits you, Andrew can bring it to your place in his truck."

"Oh, no, really, Irene, you can't do that. I'll get one of those unfinished ones."

"No, I'll have my way about this."

Thomas winked at Wynne. "You can't win an argument with Irene."

His wife wore a rather smug smile.

"Are you doing anything special for Mother's Day, Wynne?" Thomas asked.

"As a matter of fact, my sister and brother-in-law and I are going down to New Hampshire to see my folks."

"So you won't be at church Sunday?" Thomas looked a little disappointed.

"No, sorry. I'll miss you all, but it's been about six weeks since I've seen my parents, and I know they're looking forward to seeing all of us."

"Of course they are," Irene said.

"But you'll come back." Hallee looked a bit worried.

Wynne said quickly, "Of course I will. I'll see you next week."

Andy gazed at her soberly. "None of us has a mother."

Andrew's mouth skewed.

Thomas said, "Your mother's not with us right now, but we'll be with her in heaven one day."

"She loved you and Hallee very much," Irene said. "And your daddy too, of course."

135

Andy's forehead crinkled, but Hallee seemed satisfied and slathered jam on half a biscuit.

When they had finished the main meal, rhubarb pie with vanilla ice cream awaited them. What Wynne had thought would be a light lunch had turned into a feast.

While they lingered over dessert, Irene again broached the subject of the dresser. "I think I'd better send Andrew up there with you. I ate too much, and those attic stairs are too steep for me to navigate safely, anyway."

"Grandpa can show her the bureaus," Andrew said. "When she decides which one she wants, just tell me."

"No, I'm going to put those peas in this afternoon, and Andy and Hallee are going to help me." Thomas turned to Wynne apologetically. "Not that I wouldn't love to accompany you on your quest, m'dear, but I'm determined to get those peas planted."

"Really, it's too much trouble," Wynne protested. "I don't need—"

"Come on." Andrew pushed back his chair and stood up with resignation. "Gram will never let me hear the end of it if I don't get you a bureau today."

Wynne looked around at her hosts, but Thomas was already heading for the back door with the twins and Irene was smiling complacently.

"Take the best one, dear. We're not using half

the furniture in this house. Make sure it's one you like."

Andrew was halfway up the stairs, and Wynne trailed after him hesitantly. In the upstairs hallway, he strode past several doorways and opened a six-panel pine door.

"This used to be Aunt Rachel's room. My sister Phoebe had it when she was a kid."

Wynne went in and looked around at the cozy room. The wall sloped up from the eaves to meet the ceiling on one side. The soft rose wallpaper was studded with bouquets of forget-me-nots, and white organdy curtains hung at the recessed window. She could picture generations of Cook daughters feeling at home in the room.

"I couldn't take this." She put her hand out to touch the maple dresser. An oval mirror with beveled edges was mounted above it. "It's part of the bedroom set. You can't just break up a set like that."

She turned toward Andrew. He stood silently in the doorway, and she thought she saw cynicism in his steely eyes. It suddenly seemed very important to Wynne to make her motives clear.

"I really didn't intend for your grandmother to start giving me furniture. I wanted her to help me pick out something at the store—"

"She won't let you leave without one."

Wynne took a deep breath. She couldn't read

his tone, but she didn't want to offend him again. "Do you think it's right?"

He chuckled. "Right? To accept a gift from a woman who adores you?"

Her eyes flashed up to his. He was smiling slightly, and his eyes had softened.

"I love Irene," she said quietly.

"She loves you. Prays for you all the time, just like she does for us kids. It didn't take her long to make up her mind about you." He turned toward the hallway. "Next exhibit is in the attic, I guess."

He opened a door on the other side of the hall and flipped a light switch.

"It's a little dark in the stairway here. Just watch your step. It's steep."

She went past him and turned a corner, facing a flight of stairs that seemed nearly vertical.

"Can you see? Don't want you breaking a leg or something." He put his hand on her elbow, and Wynne's heart sped up. It was silly, but his gentle touch somehow made her assessment of his character more favorable. If he hated her, he wouldn't care about her wellbeing. She felt for the banister, and he followed her closely as she mounted the steps, releasing her when she stepped out onto the floor at the top.

The attic was unfinished, with rough boards on the floor and a brick chimney thrusting up between it and the underside of the roof. A single light bulb overhead shone valiantly, but most of the light came from the windows at each end of the long, narrow room.

"I think there's a bureau over here." Andrew turned to the right, and Wynne followed him carefully between piles of stored furniture, an old steamer trunk, boxes of toys, books, and dishes. He flipped a blanket back from a bulky shape. "There you go. Solid oak."

The dresser had two small drawers at the top, and two long ones below. The top two had curved fronts and brass locks.

"That mirror goes with it." Andrew nodded toward a large mirror leaning against a blanket chest. Its frame was carved oak, and the glass reflected them clearly through a layer of dust.

"It's wonderful. But I'd feel guilty—"

"You're not allowed."

She looked at him in the dim light. He was smiling, and he looked younger, much younger. Wynne wondered how she had ever found him intimidating.

He returned her look and nodded slowly. "Yup, Grammy really loves you."

"Why do you say that?" she asked, her nerves picking up something in his tone.

"Oh, sending you on this little expedition. It's not about the bureau, you know."

"It's not?" Wynne felt her contentment fleeing. "What is it about?"

He stood there for several seconds, as if

undecided how much to say. At last he chuckled. "Gram's hardly ever wrong about people."

Was he saying that she was wrong this time, or was he accepting Irene's assessment? Wynne felt uneasily that he had reached his own verdict on her, without giving her a chance to mount a defense.

"So, you want the dresser? I'll get Will to help me carry it down. When you're ready to go home, tell me, and I'll take it out to your place."

"If you're sure it's all right."

"Oh, I'm sure. If you don't take it, I'll be in hot water."

"I don't understand."

He just smiled and moved the mirror to the head of the stairs. He came back and lifted one end of the dresser, testing its weight. "Better take the drawers out, I guess."

He pulled out the top left drawer. It was full of booklets. "Looks like Gram's knitting patterns. I'll see if I can find an empty box. Want to check the other drawers?"

He rummaged under the eaves near the chimney.

Wynne hesitantly opened the top right drawer. It held a Barbie doll and several outfits.

Andrew glanced at it when he came back with a wooden box. "My sister's rubbish." He set the box down. "This will hold some stuff."

He plunked the knitting books into the crate

without ceremony, and Wynne laid the doll carefully on top.

"We ought to put it in a bag or something. It will get all dusty."

"You're right. I'll go get some plastic bags."

He went lightly down the steep steps, and Wynne opened the first long drawer of the oak dresser. She bent close to see better. Clothing, or linens. She picked up a small item and held it up to the light. Baby shoes. She smiled and began stacking the things on top of the dresser. There were two cotton baby blankets with satin binding, a pink and a blue. Two lacy bonnets. Two striped pajama suits. Bibs embroidered with "I love Grandpa," and "I love Grammy." Terrycloth suits and a frothy little pink dress.

Under all the baby clothes was a large envelope, and she lifted it out and took it over under the light bulb. There was something printed in the upper left corner, but she couldn't read it.

Andrew was coming back up the stairs, and she looked up. As he reached the top of the steps, he said, "Grammy says Lady Agatha just dropped her calf, and Grandpa wants me to take you out to see it when we're done." He stepped up beside her, holding several plastic grocery sacks. "Hey, I've been looking for that!"

"What is it?" she asked timidly, handing him the envelope.

"The kids' birth certificates. I need them to

register the twins for kindergarten in the fall. I was looking all over downstairs. Forgot they were up here, I guess."

He slid two forms from the envelope. They were covered with ornamental writing, and each had a large seal in the top left corner. Wynne could make out the names Andrew Jackson Cook II and Hallee Joyce Cook. "They're citizens of Germany and the U.S."

"These must be the twins' baby clothes, then." Wynne nodded toward the things she had piled on the dresser.

"Yup. Grammy must have put them away up here when they outgrew them." He picked up the tiny shoes. "Andy wore these on the plane. Man, that was a nightmare."

"Coming home with the babies?"

He nodded, looking at the leather shoes, and sighed deeply. When he looked up she realized she had been staring.

"Sorry." She looked away.

"It's okay. I just try not to think about it much. Don't ever try to fly across the ocean by yourself on a military transport with two screaming, week-old babies."

Wynne opened her mouth to ask, but she couldn't. His expression wrenched her heart. She wished she knew him better and could offer some comfort.

He sniffed a little.

"Andrew, I'm so sorry." She took a step toward him, then stopped. If he would accept sympathy from anyone, it wouldn't be her. He was probably wishing she had never entered the attic, or his life.

A tear rolled down his left cheek, and he wiped it away with his cuff. "Maybe I should think about it more. They hardly even know what their mother looked like."

"You must have pictures."

"A few. Gram shows them sometimes, but they don't really understand."

"They will when they're older." Wynne felt utterly helpless, and she knew tears were close for her, too.

He stood still and took a deep, ragged breath.

"What happened, Andrew?" she asked softly.

Abruptly he put the baby shoes down on the dresser and walked to the window at the far end of the room. Wynne stayed where she was, watching him bleakly, certain she had overstepped the bounds of his privacy. He stood with his hands on each side of the window frame, looking down at the barnyard.

After a few minutes, Wynne began quietly tucking the clothing into the plastic bags. She couldn't give him the empathy and love he so deeply needed, couldn't follow her instinct to put her arms around him and assure him that he was not alone in his sorrow. So she did the only thing she could to help him. The sooner their job in the attic was finished, the better.

When she was done she glanced toward him, wondering whether she should open the final drawer, or just go on downstairs and leave him alone.

"I'll bet Grammy knew that stuff was there all along."

There was an edge to his voice that made Wynne want to protect Irene from any resentment he might dredge up. "She probably just forgot."

He turned and came slowly toward her, and the light grew stronger as he stepped away from the window.

"You want to know what happened to Joyce? Near as I know, she bled to death."

"Oh, Andrew." She wished she hadn't asked.

"I was stationed over there, you know."

"Yes, Irene told me that much."

"Eighteen months." He sat down on the corner of the dresser. "Joyce wasn't due for another month. I had to go on a sortie over Croatia. Just looking, no combat. Keeping an eye on things. We had some engine trouble on the way back, and when we landed, I was just so happy to be on the ground! I was thanking God for bringing us back safe."

She nodded.

"Then a sergeant came running out with a message for me. It said to get over to the hospital pronto. I knew it was Joyce. But I didn't expect . . ." He wiped away another tear. "When I got there, they told me she was gone. She hemorrhaged, and I guess it happened real fast. They saved the babies, but Joyce was just . . . gone."

Wynne swallowed, fighting the sorrow that surged up inside her. She suspected that Andrew hadn't talked about his loss to anyone, except perhaps Thomas and Irene, and it had been more than four years, nearly five. Slowly, she put her hand out until her fingertips just touched his sleeve. "I'm so sorry."

He shuddered and shook his head slowly. "I was due to re-up, and I was going to. I was working toward being a flight instructor. Another four years, or maybe eight, and then I thought I'd get out and fly airliners. But I had those babies, and Joyce was dead, and I had to do something fast." He sighed shakily, twisting the wedding ring on his left hand.

Wynne didn't know what to say.

"I called Grandpa, and he said, 'Bring those babies home, Andy.' Nobody ever calls me Andy." He shot her a glance, with just a trace of a smile showing at the corner of his mouth.

"So you came home."

"Yes. I couldn't send the babies alone, and I had to . . . bring Joyce home, for her folks." He looked up at the chimney, then at Wynne. He had given up chasing the tears. "I thought about staying in the Air Force, but I couldn't see letting someone else raise my kids, and I knew Grammy and Grandpa were too old to do it by themselves. So I resigned my commission and became a farmer. Something I'd vowed I would never do."

"You didn't want to farm?"

"I wanted to *fly*." He shook his head. "I guess God didn't want me to."

Wynne wondered if he had accepted that edict from God with peace.

Andrew shifted, and she let her hand fall back to her side. His eyes begged for understanding. "Sometimes I think, He could have showed me some other way, you know? Oh, I know it's more than that. It's not like He killed Joyce just to make me come back here."

"A lot of people were affected by it," she ventured.

"Yeah. It's been good for Grandpa and Grammy, I think, to have us here. It's been good for Hallee and Andy too. Not as good as having a mother, maybe, but nobody could love them more than those two old people do."

"You can still be a pilot." It was the one thing he seemed capable of still having a passion for, and he was young.

"I don't know. Commercial pilots are away from home a lot."

"The children will become less dependent as they get older."

"Oh, I know, but . . ." He smiled a little, but it skewed into a grimace. "Grammy and Grandpa are old. They love the twins, but I can't expect them to take care of them for me all the time. Pretty soon they might need some care themselves."

She nodded. Cautiously she asked, "What about your in-laws? Don't they live close by? I'd think they could help out, if you went to work away from the farm."

"No way. Joyce's mother hates me."

Startled, Wynne searched his face. "You don't mean that."

"Well, she's not happy with me, that's for sure. She didn't want us to get married so young, with me going from one Air Force base to another. And she was really upset when I carted Joyce off to Europe."

Wynne saw defeat in his blue eyes. "You can't blame yourself forever."

"Can't I?"

"You didn't cause Joyce's death."

"Not directly, maybe." His jaw hardened and his eyes challenged her to prove him wrong. "After my dad died, I was pretty angry, and I wasn't thinking about anyone but myself. Over the next few years, I put the people I loved most through a lot of grief."

"How old were you when he died?"

"Sixteen." He was silent for long moment. "It seemed so senseless. How could God do that to our family?"

"Have you come to terms with that?"

"I think so, now, but it took a long time. That's why I joined the Air Force as soon as I could. I was *not* going to stay here and become the next farmer by default. One way or another, I was going to fly. My mother was heartbroken, but at that age I was too callous to realize what I was doing to the people who loved me."

"What happened to your mother?" Wynne was almost afraid to ask.

"She died four years after Dad. Cancer. I was in Texas then, training." He sighed. "Joyce was with me. She was the best thing that happened to me in all those years. I felt like she was the only person who understood me, and I wanted her with me. Her folks and my mother all tried to talk us into waiting, but I wouldn't listen."

"Joyce sided with you."

"Yeah, she'd have done anything for me. She just wanted me to be happy. So here I am."

His implication that happiness was out of his reach saddened Wynne. A man his age ought to have a built-in optimism, no matter what sorrow the past had dealt him.

So, how happy am I?

Since moving back to Maine, Wynne had

struggled with insecurity, fatigue and loneliness. Even though her sister was within reach, happiness seemed to elude her. She might catch it one day, if she was patient and did everything right.

She wanted Andrew to be happy, too, and irrationally in that moment his happiness seemed somehow tied to hers. She cared about him and his family, and she knew that she would do anything she could to bolster him. But for now, it seemed she couldn't do anything but pray for him. He would not accept more than that.

He shrugged and hopped down off the dresser. "Let's get this thing unloaded."

"Let's."

He took hold of the brass drawer pulls on the bottom drawer and pulled it open. His uniforms lay neatly folded, the buttons and decorations gleaming in the feeble beam of the overhead light.

Wynne laid her hand on his arm as he bent to lift them out. "I think your family needs this dresser."

"That's silly. These can go in a box." He looked around, then opened the old steamer trunk that stood near the window. "There's plenty of room in here with Aunt Rachel's petticoats." He took a stack of clothing from the drawer and carried it to the trunk.

Wynne gave up and lifted out the last of the clothing. Andrew unclasped the silver wings from the front of his dress uniform. He met her eyes gravely as he tucked them in his shirt pocket.

"Let's go see that calf. Will and I will get the dresser later."

He went ahead of her down the stairs and turned around, holding out his arm toward her in case she missed her footing. He turned off the light and closed the attic door, and they went on down to the first floor. The large, sunny rooms were empty. He stopped Wynne in the living room and picked at something in her hair.

"Cobweb," he said with smile.

She laughed. "Am I as filthy as you are?"

"I guess not." He held her gaze for a long moment. "Thanks, Wynne."

"For what?"

"For listening, I guess. I think I needed to face all of that again. And Grammy—she was definitely right about you."

"Daddy, Daddy," Hallee cried when they entered the barn. She ran to Andrew and flung herself at him.

Andrew swung her up in his arms and carried her to where Thomas, Irene, and Andy stood admiring the new Jersey calf.

"What should his name be?" Andy asked, stroking the baby's damp flank. Lady Agatha was licking the calf's neck with her broad pink tongue.

"It's a bull calf?" Andrew asked, looking at his grandfather.

"Afraid so. He goes out on the truck Thursday."

"Not worth naming, then."

"He ought to have a name while he's here, Daddy," Hallee pleaded.

"Foolishness," said Thomas.

"Oh, let her," Andrew relented, and Wynne thought the tenderness she had seen in the attic was lingering.

"Let's name him Mr. Bureau," said Hallee.

They all laughed. "Bureau isn't a name," Irene said.

"Yes it is," Hallee insisted. "Mr. Bureau at the farm store."

"She's right," Thomas chuckled. "Paul Bureau gave her a lollipop a month ago, and she won't forget it."

"And Miss Harding is getting a bureau from the attic today," Andy reminded them.

"Or we could name him Attic," said Hallee.

"Let's stick with Mr. Bureau." Andrew's glance touched Wynne, and she smiled. "Speaking of bureaus, I need to get Will to help me take that thing down from the attic, or I won't get back before milking time."

"You don't have to bring it today," Wynne said.

He checked his watch. "Well, how about after supper? Would that be all right? Will and I can load it now, then I'll milk, and I'll come out there with it later."

Wynne left the barn with Irene and put her arm around her as they walked toward her hatchback in the driveway.

"Irene, thank you for making this day special for me. I had so much fun in town with you this morning, and lunch was great—"

"And you're getting your bureau," Irene concluded.

"Yes, and I think you should know that Andrew thinks you've put one over on us, sending us up to the attic together."

"I wouldn't know how to 'put one over,' as you say," Irene protested.

"Oh, wouldn't you just?" Wynne laughed. The fact that Andrew hadn't seemed to mind too much took away any resentment she might have felt.

Irene's white eyebrows rose. "But the two of you are speaking now."

"Yes, we're speaking. Do you know what we found in the dresser drawers?"

"Andrew said he'd found my knitting books and his sister's doll."

"Well, it was more than that. I'll let Andrew tell you about it if he wants to." She bent and kissed Irene's smooth cheek. "You are a dear."

Chapter 10

Wynne was watching out the window for Andrew's pickup when her sister called at half past six. Hearing Rebecca's vibrant voice reminded her of the trip they had planned for Sunday.

"Hi, Wynne. Are you all set for Mother's Day?"

"I think so. What time do you want me at your place?" Wynne planned to drive that far and leave her car in their driveway.

"Rob's willing to leave as early as you want. Want to try for seven?"

"Mom and Dad won't get home from church until noon."

"That's right. Let's say eight then."

"I think I can manage that." Wynne wouldn't have to get up any earlier than she did on a workday. The four-hour drive would put them at their parents' house around noon, and they'd have time for a good visit. "Now, tell me about the ribbon cutting."

"It was very nice. They paid tribute to Rob and the builder, as well as the partners in the medical practice. And they gave a tour and served refreshments. Oh, guess who I saw today?"

"Who?"

"Wade Pierce," Rebecca said.

Wynne blinked. The boy from her high school class had been her crush during her junior year, but Wade had never asked her out. When he latched on to a girlfriend, she'd mourned deeply. She'd been accepted at three colleges, and she chose the one where Wade was studying. To no avail. Wade was a year ahead of her, and when she saw him sporadically, he would barely acknowledge her presence.

"Are you struck dumb?" Rebecca asked.

"Not exactly."

"He asked about you."

"You're kidding."

"Nope. He said, 'How's your sister doing?' When I told him you were back in the area, making your name as a journalist, he was suitably impressed."

"Did he say if he's married?"

"That's the best part. His girlfriend broke the engagement. He's still single."

"I'm overcome," Wynne said without a trace of emotion.

"Think about it." Rebecca was buoyant. "You pine for him for years, and he ignores you."

"I didn't."

"Sure you did. Then he gets engaged to someone else. You go away and mend your broken heart, his engagement gets smashed, and, presto, he thinks of you."

"Oh, please. I didn't pine for him for years, and

I didn't go away to mend my heart." She realized Rebecca didn't know Wade took his engineering degree at the same college she'd attended—and she wasn't going to tell her. Quickly, she said, "And today, he only thought of me because he saw you. I'm sure there was nothing more to it than that."

"No, he asked me if you were married. I told him you're not, but that a state trooper is madly pursuing you."

"I shouldn't have mentioned Dave the last time we talked," Wynne said ruefully.

"I didn't tell him about the spitting part, or that you brushed him off," Rebecca assured her.

"Well, yesterday I did more than that. I did something that put him off me for good."

"What? Jaywalked?"

"No, I told him I only date believers. He never wants to see me again."

"Wow," Rebecca said softly. "Sorry, hon."

"No great loss, as far as my love life goes. I wish he would have listened, though."

"Aren't there any guys at the depot-with-a-steeple?"

"It's a really small church."

"Wade is going for his MBA."

"What? You mean he's given up on engineering?"

"Guess so. I don't know what happened, but he told me he switched his major to business after two years in college. Now he wants the master's, so he's going back to school this summer."

Wynne decided it was time to change the subject. "What's going on with you and Rob?" A sound outside drew her gaze to the front window. "Oops! I've got to go. A man is delivering my new dresser. He just drove in."

"Okay. You can tell me about *that* on Sunday."

Wynne opened the front door. Andrew, in clean jeans and a chambray shirt, was opening the tailgate of his truck. She could see comb strokes in his damp hair, and his genuine smile sent a thrill through her. Maybe they were past the prickly stage. She'd have to be careful what she told Rebecca during their road trip, or her sister would pester her constantly for details.

"Hi." Andrew had lowered the tailgate and was already in the bed of the pickup. "I think you're going to have to help me. This thing is pretty heavy."

"No problem. Just let me get my shoes."

She scrambled for her sneakers and looked around quickly to make sure everything was neat.

They carried in the drawers first and stacked them on the floor by her bed, the only piece of furniture in the bedroom until that moment. Her suitcase and clothes boxes were hidden in the closet. The living room was nearly as bare.

"You've been living a Spartan existence,"

Andrew said as he lowered the ornate mirror onto her quilt.

"Well, I couldn't bring much with me."

"I'm glad this piece of furniture is going to a good cause."

They went out one more time to get the dresser. The sun on the western horizon intensified the greens of grass and new leaves. The oak dresser gleamed, and Wynne ran her hand over the golden wood. In the attic, it had sat, dusty and neglected, a utilitarian piece of furniture. In the brilliant light, she could see its beauty, coaxed to a sheen by loving hands that had polished it since she'd left the farm.

"It's beautiful."

Andrew smiled, and Wynne felt something unknot inside her. The change she was seeing in Andrew, though slow in coming, was as striking as that of the antique dresser.

He slid it across the old bedspread he had placed under it in the truck. "Not a scratch on it."

They lowered it gently, and Andrew walked backward, with Wynne at the other end walking forward. Together they carried the heavy piece to the steps, then carefully up and into the house.

"Set it down for a minute," Andrew said in the kitchen.

Wynne was glad for the respite. "They don't make them like this anymore."

"You got that right."

"I'll give you a glass of lemonade when we're done."

"Great. Ready?" They bent to the task again, and soon had the dresser in the bedroom.

"I brought a screwdriver so I can put the mirror on for you," Andrew said.

"Oh, thanks." She didn't have any tools, and she'd have been stymied if he hadn't thought of it.

While he attached the mirror, Wynne poured lemonade and put a bag of popcorn in the microwave. He came from the bedroom tucking the screwdriver into a pocket.

"All done."

"Thank you so much. Do you like popcorn?"

"The high-cholesterol microwave kind?"

"Yes."

"Love it. Grammy won't let it in the house. Too much salt, too many chemicals, she says. She makes it the old-fashioned way, in a pan on the stove."

"I'll bet it's just as good."

"Maybe, but it's different." He sat down at the table, picked up one of the frosty glasses, and took a long drink.

"So, when's your birthday?"

"My birthday?" She was suddenly self-conscious.

"You said this afternoon you were born in May."

"I was."

"So, when is it?" He tossed a piece of popcorn into the air and caught it in his mouth.

Wynne laughed. "You're just like my dad. I bet you'd get along great."

"You're avoiding the question. It's not today, is it?"

"No, May thirtieth."

"Memorial Day?"

"That's right, when it falls on the right day. I was eight years old before I figured out the parade wasn't for me."

He smiled. "Did you always go to the parade?"

"Every year. My folks made a really big deal over it. We'd take a picnic and go watch the parade and listen to one of the oldest veterans read the Gettysburg Address, and then they fire the cannon. When the ceremony was over, we'd walk around in the cemetery, putting flowers on the graves of all our family that's buried there."

"That would be the cemetery here in Belgrade, right? You said your family lived here."

"Yes. My brother-in-law's family makes a big deal of Memorial Day, too. I'll probably celebrate with the Hardings this year."

"The Hardings? You don't mean—wait a sec. Is your sister married to Rob Wallace?"

"Yeah. Do you know him?"

"He was a year behind me in school. His dad has the hardware store."

"That's right. He and Rebecca got married last fall."

"Well, I'll be."

"I'll miss being with my folks," Wynne said. "But I'll see them Sunday. My dad wants to move back up here when he retires."

"When will that be?"

"Two or three more years, I think. He hasn't said for sure." She sipped her drink, looking at him over the rim of the glass.

He picked up his glass, and the ice clinked. "Do you like being a reporter?"

The question was unexpected, and Wynne hesitated, wondering if he really cared, and if she knew the answer. "Most of the time. Not always. I don't like thinking I'm not strong enough or tough enough, but sometimes the stories they send me to cover . . ." She shook her head.

"What would you rather do?"

"I don't know. I wouldn't want to just do the social page all the time or be the formatter or . . ." She shook her head. "I actually liked my coworkers better at the little weekly where I worked in New Hampshire, but that was just part time. I couldn't really make anything, and I didn't want my dad to support me all my life."

Andrew started to speak, but her phone rang. She set down her lemonade and picked it up. "That's my sister, Rebecca."

"I'd better get going, anyway." Andrew stood up.

"Thanks a lot for bringing the dresser."

"Anytime."

He went out the door with a little wave, and she swiped her phone.

"Wynne, where were you? I was beginning to think the delivery man had made away with you."

She turned away from the door, pushing down all thoughts of Andrew. She would analyze her feelings later. "Hi, Rebecca. What's up?"

"I just wanted to know what you're taking to Mom. We got her a plant and a gift card."

"That's nice. I got her some earrings and a box of Maine stationery."

"She'll love those."

"I hope so."

"So, should I give Wade your phone number?"

"No thanks."

"Are you sure there aren't any prospects up there, other than the cop?"

"Well, I'm not sure it's a prospect, but there is a guy . . ." Wynne was startled at her own words. Andrew Cook had not made her edgy during his brief visit. Instead, she realized she had enjoyed talking to him very much. Still, she wasn't sure she should tell Rebecca about him yet. There was nothing to tell, really.

"What's he like?" Rebecca asked eagerly.

Too late. Wynne took a deep breath. "He's . . . a widower."

"What! I suppose he's Dad's age and has teen-aged children."

"No, he's twenty-eight. He has four-year-old twins."

"Didn't we hear something about twins before?"

"Yes, the same ones. Andy and Hallee."

"I thought you had their father cast as a villain."

"I just didn't know him, is all."

"And now you do, and he's Prince Charming."

"Not exactly. Look, I don't know him very well yet, but he's interesting, okay? You asked me if there was anyone out there, and so far that's about it. Oh, and he knows Rob."

"Really? What's his name?"

There was no getting out of it now. "Andrew Cook."

"I'll pick Rob's brain and see what he knows about him."

"It might be more fun to let me find out for myself."

Rebecca chuckled. "Okay. I'd better get going. I'm really glad you're going with us Sunday."

Wynne finished her workday at five the following Wednesday, and she slipped into the church just as the Bible study opened. She took a seat in the row behind the Cooks. She hadn't seen them for a week, and she'd hoped to be able to catch up on

162

things with them afterward, but she wasn't able to avoid the spotlight.

Her article about the church had appeared in that morning's paper, with the photo of the building being moved and another of a crane raising the steeple. When the service ended, the congregation crowded around her.

"You did a super job," Ray Harder said, pumping her hand. "We're all proud of you."

Wynne smiled, wishing she could avoid the attention. "Thanks. I enjoyed working on it. It was the kind of story that's fun to write—no angry people, and nobody hurt."

"You're an excellent writer," Tracy Marks said.

"Thank you, you're very kind." Wynne's face was flaming, and she wished the article had appeared on a day when there was no service.

Irene grasped her arm. "Thomas went to the store and bought a dozen copies, so we can send them to all the grandchildren." As they gathered their things to go home, she said, "Thomas and the kids took me out to eat Sunday, for Mother's Day, and Phoebe and her family came up. It was a nice day."

"I enjoyed my visit with my folks too," Wynne said.

"I'm glad. Andrew took the twins to see his mother-in-law, before supper."

"Where do they live?"

Thomas leaned in. "They're just up the road

about a mile from us. It's the next big farm."

"So, he married the girl next door?" She watched Andrew snap Hallee's helmet strap under her chin.

"Just about," Thomas agreed.

"They don't go to church here," Wynne observed.

"No, they've always gone over to Smithfield." Thomas and Irene kept pace with her as they walked out to the parking lot. "You come to dinner with us on Sunday, okay?"

"Well, I—"

Irene eyed her sternly. "Please do. You have a standing invitation with us."

Wynne smiled, but she had noted that Andrew kept aloof that evening, in spite of the strides they had made on their foray to the attic the week before. "All right, if you're sure no one will mind."

Thomas's eyebrows quirked. "Don't tell me that boy's been rude to you. I'll—"

"No, no! He hasn't. It's just—well, sometimes he seems uncomfortable around me." She wished she hadn't said anything. Thomas and Irene were obviously perturbed, and she regretted causing that.

Thomas's brow furrowed. "He's had a bad experience with reporters, but still, that's no excuse."

Wynne grasped the sleeve of his sweater.

"Please don't say anything to him. It's all right." Thomas shook his head in exasperation, but Wynne said again, "Please."

The old man's eyes had lost their usual sparkle. "All right, we'll let it go."

Wynne had grown comfortable with the software at the newspaper office, and she could now write and file her articles efficiently without asking for help. She took a little good-natured teasing about Dave Workman in the office, but she let Julie know she had sent the policeman packing, and the word soon filtered around.

"What about the farmer?" Julie asked, but Wynne had no intention of making Andrew an object of gossip, and said only, "He's still farming."

Julie chuckled. "Hey, did you hear about Jim?"

"Jim Dowdy? No, what about him?"

"He's quitting. Going to the *Boston Globe*."

"No way."

"Uh-huh."

Wynne sat staring at her screen for at least half a minute. What would this mean to the remaining reporters at the *Guardian*?

"I've been reading in the book you brought me," Julie told her at lunch on Friday. "I bought a Bible, too."

"That's great."

"It's making me feel really guilty, though."

"What for?"

"Just for being me. The chapter I finished last night in the study book was about how everybody has sinned. And it made sense. That's the scary part!"

"Well, keep reading," Wynne said. "You'll soon get to the part about redemption. That's why Jesus came to earth, to die for those sins."

Julie's eyebrows drew together. "I never really understood what the cross had to do with it. How could dying like that save someone else?"

Wynne chose her words carefully. "The Bible says God *made him, who knew no sin, to be sin for us.* Jesus could take our punishment because he was innocent."

Julie frowned and walked to the trash can with her sandwich wrapper. "I don't know . . ."

"Keep reading."

"Okay, but right now I've got two honor rolls to type in."

Wynne wanted to ask if she'd heard any rumors about who would take over Jim's police beat, but she kept quiet. She wouldn't mind doing more city hall stories, but the crime end of things made her uneasy. Would she be cast in a role that would have her researching and writing the details of violent crimes for the next several years? She crumpled her sandwich wrapper and tossed it in the trash.

Chapter 11

On Saturday, Wynne drove to her second graduation. This one was held inside, and although the slow-moving ceremony turned out to be quite tedious, the main speaker was lively enough to hold Wynne's interest and give her some palatable quotes. She glimpsed Ken Ricker once, sneaking up the steps of the platform to get a close-up. She tiptoed out as the diplomas were distributed.

By four thirty, she was in the office typing rapidly. Ken came in and called a greeting to her as he sat down to load his photos into the system. A copy editor had come in for the evening by the time she had finished her article and was ready to review her story. She went home and collapsed on the couch.

Still no word on reassigning Jim Dowdy's regular beat. He'd be working in Waterville another week, and then he'd be off to Boston. Would they hire a new reporter? She'd heard rumblings about downsizing and budget constraints. Maybe they would all have to carry the load of the extra work once Jim left.

She opened her refrigerator and stared inside for ten seconds, then sighed and closed it.

A call to her mother might help. Wynne placed

the call, and hearing her mom's loving voice soothed her a little, but didn't lift her spirits much. After they'd signed off, she decided to get out of the house.

The town's park was practically deserted, and she realized it was suppertime for most people. She parked and sat on a bench in the sun for a while, until two cars pulled in and shouting children spilled out. She should have gone down to Rebecca's. If she had, she could be out on the lake right now in Rob's canoe.

A cemetery lay nearby, shaded by mature oaks and sugar maples. Wynne walked through it slowly, stopping often to read inscriptions. At last she came to a wrought iron bench near a large monument with an angel perched on the top, and she sat down, shivering a little as a cloud covered the sun.

The lettering carved on the stone monument read: "Herman A. Jelliman, He loved all and was loved by all." Her gaze followed the obelisk up to the angel, and beyond it to the sky.

How would she be remembered when she left this earth? "Wynne M. Harding, beloved daughter, competent reporter, struggling Christian." Maybe she was being too generous to herself. How about a simple "Wynne M. Harding, failure"?

She pulled her legs up and sat hugging her knees. She'd had discouraging days before, but this was an all-time low. She recognized the effects of loneliness and conflict.

Dave Workman's sneering hostility still stung. Speaking of her faith had been much easier with Julie, but she'd liked Julie to begin with. Maybe that's why God put me here, she thought. Maybe no one else would have told them about Christ.

Tomorrow would be better. She'd go to church with the Cooks, and then she'd drive to her sister's house for lunch. She'd told Irene she had promised Rebecca, and she knew she'd enjoy the afternoon there. Her sister could always cheer her up.

She thought of Andrew, and his crushed dreams. His family was shattered, his aspirations dashed. She had tried to encourage him, but she couldn't see much improvement in his outlook. If only she had met him at another time, when he wasn't fighting such a fierce inner battle. Maybe his melancholia was pulling her down. Probably it was best that she wouldn't be spending tomorrow at the farm.

She was startled by the regret that shot through her. Andrew was a man you couldn't get close to unless he allowed it to happen. In the attic, for a few minutes, he had opened the door to his soul a crack, but she wondered if he wished he hadn't.

A cold breeze picked up, and she got up and walked through the cemetery to the parking lot. As she drove home, she struggled with the fact that she cared deeply for Andrew. It hurt to think that their relationship might never be more than tolerance on his part. Did he resent his grandparents' pulling her into the family circle?

She prayed, *Do I really belong here, Lord? The job, the church . . . Maybe I should quit going to the Cooks' church.* But she doubted that would make her feel better.

The job was a more practical concern. She'd thought she would love reporting, but her work at the *Guardian* didn't bring her the satisfaction she'd anticipated. Even when people praised her writing, she felt she hadn't done well enough.

I can stay at the paper, Father, if that's where you want me, but I need your help. I want to feel at home in the place where I go to work every day. And Andrew . . . She let out a long sigh. *Don't let me set my heart on something I can never have.*

Everyone at the office seemed to think Jim was brilliant and had proven his genius by snagging a job at a big city paper. Staffers stopped frequently at his desk to congratulate him. On Thursday, they threw him a farewell party at noon.

While most of her coworkers were eating cake, Chuck Barnes strolled casually over to Wynne. "You'll be taking over Jim's city hall beat. Get the police log tomorrow, and touch base with the district attorney on the Stratton case. That's yours now. I told Jim to give you his notes. " He walked on and called, "Okay, people, back to work."

Wynne stared after him. She considered all her options carefully before approaching him an hour later. If he insisted, she would accept the assignment and go to the police station the next day, but she figured it wouldn't hurt to make it known she didn't want the assignment. When she saw him hang up his telephone receiver, she walked over and stood beside his desk.

"Chuck?"

"Yeah?" He didn't look up from the papers he was scanning.

"I was wondering—I know Jim's leaving and all, but—" She faltered to a stop, and he looked up at last.

"What?"

"Is there any way you could have someone else do this story?"

"What, the child pornography case?"

She nodded. "I've only been to the police station once, and I haven't handled any crime stories. I've never been to a trial, and I'm really nervous about it."

"You gotta learn sometime." He went back to work.

She stood still, trying frantically to come up with an excuse or an argument.

Chuck glanced up again. "Are you still here? We have deadlines."

"I know, but—Deedee—"

He tossed down the sheaf of papers and glared at her. "If I wanted Deedee to write this story, I'd have assigned it to Deedee. What's the problem? Are you sick?"

"No." She wished desperately that she were.

"Do you think you can't handle it? Because I say you can."

Wynne swallowed. It was the closest he had ever come to praising her work, and she wasn't sure he had meant it that way. "I just don't feel comfortable with the topic."

Chuck sighed. "Nobody likes the topic. Only a sicko would enjoy covering it. But we have to present it to the public in an accurate, even-handed manner. With that said, please do your job."

Wynne nodded and turned away, more nervous than before. As she headed for the stairway, Chuck called after her, "And I'll expect you to get the arraignment in the morning. Be at District Court when they take him in."

She drove to the police station through pounding rain the next morning and collapsed her red umbrella inside the lobby. She approached the front desk, her stomach roiling.

"Hi, I'm here from the paper, about the Stratton case, and I'll need to see the police log." Her clammy skirt clung to her calves.

The desk officer took her to where they kept

the log book, and she quickly made notes on the entries for the last two days. As she walked back to the desk, the street door opened and a man in a suit ducked inside, shaking his umbrella before he folded it.

"Miss Harding."

She looked up into Deputy Chief Parker's face. His glasses were fogging, and he pulled them off. "Is someone helping you?"

"I'm here about the Stratton case."

Parker frowned. "Not a very pleasant job. Come, let me introduce you to our detective sergeant." He stepped to the doorway beyond the dispatchers' window and punched in the code on the keypad.

Wynne followed him into the inner hallway, grateful to have his authority on her side.

"How's it going for you at the *Guardian*?"

"I'm learning."

He paused and looked into her eyes. "I'm guessing you're not crazy about this assignment."

"I hate this assignment. It scares me to death."

"Detective Sergeant Williams is very thorough. He'll help you any way he can."

"Thank you, sir."

Parker stepped to an open doorway and gave a token knock on the panel. "Len, we've got a reporter for the *Guardian* here, on the Stratton file. This is Miss Harding. She's inexperienced and a little nervous, but she's very good if you treat her right." He winked at her and went off down the hall.

Wynne could hardly believe the change in his attitude toward her. She stepped forward, clearing her throat. Williams stood up and smiled, putting her immediately at ease. His hair was graying, and she guessed he was near retirement age. He reminded her of one of her journalism professors, and she found it hard to imagine him leaning over a corpse or handcuffing a drug dealer. She sat down with her damp notebook in her lap.

"This is the kind of case we dread, Miss Harding, but at the same time we're glad to act on it, because it means we're taking a very dangerous man off the streets of Waterville."

She nodded. "It's going to shock our readers to learn this man was producing pornographic materials right here in town."

He sat down in his swivel chair. "Unfortunately, my squad has been dealing with it every day for some time now. We've been working on this case for about four months. I'll give you the facts of the arrest we made this morning, and then you can ask me questions."

Wynne began writing rapidly as he detailed the case, thankful for an interview subject who was coherent. Williams was obviously an old hand, and he made her job quite easy, despite the sensitive topic.

After twenty minutes, she felt she had a good

grasp of the situation. Williams leaned back in his chair with an encouraging smile.

"So, anything else?"

"I admire you and your detectives for doing this job. Doesn't it bother you to handle cases like this?"

He sighed. "To be honest, some days it's very depressing. We get something really disgusting, and I feel as if I'll contaminate my family when I go home."

"How do you cope with that?"

He hesitated, shifting in his chair, then met her eyes. "God gets me through it."

She caught her breath. "You're a Christian?"

"Yes. Without God, I'd have burned out on this job long ago. It's the only thing that keeps me going."

"What about officers who don't believe in God?"

He frowned. "Some people can't do this job, period. Others can take it for a while, then they need a change. We're always alert to the psychological effects this type of work has on the officers, and we try to help them with that. We have professional counseling available at all times."

Wynne nodded. "I guess I'm really thinking of myself, Sergeant. Since I started this job, I've mostly handled mundane stories. But this one makes my skin crawl. And sometimes I get sent out to an accident or something. I see people suffer, and I'm not sure that's good for me or the readers. I mean, what good will this story do?"

"This specific story, on the arrest we made this morning?"

"Yes. I hate doing it, and I wonder why I should do it."

"Maybe you should have asked for another assignment."

"I did."

"I see."

"Our police reporter, Jim Dowdy, is leaving us for the *Boston Globe*. The city editor told me to come. If I want to keep my job, I can't refuse to do stories he gives me. So I do it, and I try very hard to do it well. But it makes me feel sick."

Williams folded his hands on his desk and remained silent for a moment. "Well, I'm sorry you had to come, but carrying through on it will certainly help you grow as a reporter. Maybe you personally shouldn't be the one to write this type of story, but I believe your sensitivity will be an asset, and what you write will do a lot of good."

Wynne sat up straighter. "Can you tell me how? Because that might help me." She realized she'd been struggling with her career choice since taking the job at the *Guardian*.

It wasn't just the emotional upheaval she experienced when covering stories of violence. It was the need to prove—to whom, she wasn't sure—her parents, her boss, herself—that she could succeed. The humiliation of admitting she might have made a bad decision also dragged her down. The thought of the money her parents had poured into her education was another factor.

The sergeant met her gaze. "For starters, you're alerting the public to what's going on in this town. The people need to know. It's possible that, as a result of your article, more victims will come forward to testify against Stratton. That would help keep him where he can't hurt more children. It may also wake up some parents to the dangers their children face."

"You have children." She nodded toward one of the photos on his desk. It showed him with a woman she assumed was his wife and three youngsters.

"Yes, and grandchildren. I want very much to see this man imprisoned for life."

"I want that, too, after the things you've told me he's done, but . . ." She smiled in apology as tears flooded her eyes. "I'm sorry, Sergeant. I'm taking up your time, agonizing over my own situation, and that's not fair." She stood up.

"No problem." Williams reached out to shake her hand. "Call me if you need any more information. And, Miss Harding, it's not a crime to change jobs."

She raised her eyebrows. "I admit I'm leery of what people would think."

"Don't be. Pray about it, and consider your options. You may decide to stick with it, but if you don't, it's all right."

"Thank you for saying that."

He smiled. "Not everybody here knows this, but twenty years ago, I was a landscaper."

"Really? What made you go into police work?"

"My kids. I wanted to keep them safe. Mine and everybody else's."

"Have you been able to do that?"

"I realized a long time ago that I can't do it alone. But, by the grace of God, we've had enough successes to keep me at it."

Chapter 12

"Tough story Wynne wrote this time." Thomas shook his head and sipped his coffee while reading the front section of the paper.

Irene began clearing the breakfast dishes. "I don't even want to read it. The headline alone will give me nightmares."

Frowning, Andrew pulled on his rubber boots at the back door. Grandpa always took Wynne's side. "You know she doesn't have to do that."

Thomas lowered the paper. "Of course she does."

"She told me the day we went to town that she gets assignments, and she doesn't feel she can refuse them," Irene said staunchly.

"She's only been there a couple of months. She shouldn't be covering stuff like that."

Thomas drained his coffee cup. "They give the tough stories to the best writers."

"That's a myth, Grandpa."

Thomas stood up and scowled at him, and Andrew immediately felt sorry for arguing with the man he loved so much.

"What are you saying?" Thomas asked. "That Wynne wanted to write about that—that—child molester?" He put on his cap and reached for his jacket as Andrew zipped his slicker.

"All I'm saying is, if she wanted to get out of it

badly enough, she could have found a way. But she didn't."

Dodging puddles on the way to the barn, they didn't speak. Unwelcome thoughts churned in Andrew's mind. Like the fact that he liked Wynne Harding very much, more than he'd ever liked any woman other than Joyce.

If anyone had asked him, he'd have said Wynne wasn't his type, but now he was wondering if he even knew what his "type" was. He'd known Joyce all his life, and loving her had seemed natural. He couldn't say that about Wynne. It was very unsettling to find his attraction to her growing unbidden.

Once inside the milk room, they stripped off their wet coats and hung them on hooks. Thomas turned to face him with a trace of belligerence in his face, and Andrew could see that he still felt compelled to defend Wynne.

"She's a terrific writer."

"I didn't say she's not, Grandpa. But she could use her talents in a better way."

"She's writing truth."

Andrew sighed. "Think about it. What's she having to do to get this story?"

"Well, I suppose she talked to the police about it."

"Yes, and she probably read their reports too. She's had to wade through a lot of material to sift out what should go in her article."

"That's right."

"I don't know about you, but I don't want to earn my living poring over what some filthy scum does to earn his." Andrew hefted one of the portable milking machines and headed for the door.

"Well, she's a very good friend of mine and Irene's, and you'd better not do anything to upset her."

Andrew stopped, wincing at his injured tone. "I won't, Gramp."

Thomas shook his head. "I don't understand why you don't like her. She's a wonderful girl."

"I like her. I don't like what she does. As a person, she's fine."

"She's got to support herself." Thomas grabbed the second milking machine, but stopped suddenly, standing rigid, one hand on the machine.

"Grandpa, you okay?" Andrew set down the milker and hurried to his side. "What's wrong?"

"I'm all right."

"You're not getting sick on me, are you?"

Thomas grimaced. "No, I'm not sick."

Andrew unclenched his grandfather's hand and set the equipment aside. "Come on, you'd better sit."

"No, I'm not going to sit. If I sit, I may never get up again." Thomas pushed ineffectively at Andrew and grimaced, his face turning gray.

"What hurts?" Andrew was afraid now. Was it his heart? "Grandpa, talk to me!"

"It's just old age, son."

"Oh, is that what the doctor calls it?"

"It's my back. Arthritis, most likely, or lumbago, or some such thing."

"You're seeing a doctor. Today."

Very slowly, Thomas straightened, putting both hands to his lower back. "My body's just tired, that's all."

Andrew nodded grimly. "Well, it's high time you quit doing this. Where's Will, anyhow? He should have been here by now. You shouldn't be lugging the milking machine around."

"Will's taking today off, remember?"

"He's not the only one." Andrew took Thomas's jacket from the hook. "Put this back on. You're going in the house."

"Oh, you're going to milk single-handed today?"

"I'll call Bob and see if one of the boys can come help me."

Thomas shook his head. "They're more short-handed than we are."

"Well, I can't milk any cows if I have to babysit you!" Andrew spoke sharply, more from fear than anger. He made an effort to calm his voice. "Come on, Grandpa."

Thomas stuck his arm in the jacket sleeve meekly.

"I'm sorry. I'm just tired."

"Tired and stubborn. Gramp, it's time we made some changes around here."

"Past time."

"What, you agree with me?"

Thomas smiled. "Well, now. I've been wondering how long it would take you to come out of this slump. What kind of changes are we going to make?"

Andrew eyed him warily. "Well, for starters, you shouldn't be milking anymore, or lifting hay bales, either."

"Great."

"Oh, yeah?"

"Yeah. I've been trying to retire for ten or fifteen years, but life keeps getting in the way."

"You serious?"

"You bet I'm serious. I was going to sell out and retire five years ago, remember?"

Andrew stood back and tried to read any hidden meanings, but it was clear what his grandfather meant. "I didn't mean to keep you from doing what you wanted, Grandpa." His voice broke.

"I know." Thomas clapped a hand on his shoulder. "It wasn't your fault. Those little tykes needed a place to live, and I couldn't see any other way to keep food on the table at the time. So we just kept on doing what we'd been doing."

"I should have taken a job in town." Andrew felt a bit dazed.

"Not with the twins so tiny, and no mother. They needed you here. They needed all of us.

And we gave them what they needed, the three of us together."

"I needed you too."

"And we needed you." Thomas said. "I can't picture how boring the last five years would have been without you and those little ones. Irene and I would probably be holed up in some retirement home, playing canasta."

Andrew barked a laugh. "It'll never happen."

"Well, we came mighty close."

"Is that what you and Gram want?"

"No, but we were counting on some time to relax together when we hit the upper age bracket."

Andrew leaned on the milk tank. "So, what do we do now?"

"Well, I had it figured pretty close then. Irene and I could live on the money from the farm and the herd, provided we neither one of us lived past a hundred and ten."

Andrew smiled. "You want to sell out now?"

Thomas shrugged. "Is that so shocking?"

"I guess not. It's just . . . well, this has been our home so long. Four generations. I never really think about the family without the farm."

Thomas pulled in a long breath. "I know. For a long time, I figured your father would have the place, and Irene and I would build a little house down in the lower pasture, at the edge of the woods, for our retirement. But Andy's gone, and you don't want to farm all your life—"

"I'll stay as long as you need me, Grandpa." He meant it. If these dear people needed him to farm for the next twenty years, he'd do it. Even so, he wouldn't be able to repay them for all they'd done for him and the twins.

"I know you will. That means a lot. I guess we should give some thought to what's best for the family now."

"Well, I know one thing. What's best for you is to get you in the house and let Gram take care of you."

"It's this rain," Thomas grumbled. "I always ache more when it rains."

Wynne had sloshed from assignment to assignment with her umbrella all week. In addition to her crime story, she wrote articles about a school fair, an industrial accident, an upcoming political meeting, and school board policy.

Her week culminated with the interview of sixty-year-old triplets and a college graduation that was longer than the first one she'd covered. It was held outside on the athletic field, and thousands sat miserably in a mist, shivering and willing the administrators to speed things up.

She was soaked to the skin when she got back to the office, and she sneezed irregularly as she typed. Her damp hair stuck to her cheeks and neck, and her wet clothes clung clammily.

Ken came from the editor's desk with his camera in his hand. "You look like a drowned rat."

Wynne sneezed.

"Better go home and drink something hot and go to bed."

"I have seven inches of copy to go."

"You sound horrible. It's probably what Jerry had last week. He was in here sneezing all over the place. I told him to go home, but it was too late."

"I think I'm going to be really sick," she moaned.

"Do you have any cold medicine at home?"

"No."

Ken rifled his desk drawers and brought over a package of generic cold pills.

"Take these. They've been sitting in my desk since my last cold."

"Do they work?"

"If you think they do, they do."

"Thanks."

It was nearly eight o'clock when she got home and stumbled into the shower, then pulled on sweatpants and a UNH sweatshirt and crawled shivering into bed beneath the warm quilt.

She called Irene in the morning, before Sunday School.

"I knew you'd be worried about me. It's just a cold, but I need to stay in bed, I think."

"I'm sorry, dear. We'll miss you."

"Excuse me." Wynne turned away from the phone and sneezed three times. "I just need to rest."

"Of course. Drink lots of liquids, and stay warm. We'll pray for you."

She slept most of the day, crawling out of bed a few times to drink juice or tea and take Ken's pills. They seemed to help a little and allowed her to sleep for a while before she awoke all stuffed up again.

On Monday morning, she called the office as soon as she thought Chuck would be in.

"I'm really sick. You don't want me there."

"You're right," Chuck replied. "Do you want to take a sick day, or would you rather make this your day off and work Saturday?"

"Do I have a choice?"

"Well, Ken told me you had a rough time Saturday."

"If it's all right with you, I'll take a sick day. If I can possibly come in tomorrow, I will. I promise."

"All right, I'll expect you. Deedee can get the high school graduation Saturday."

She felt marginally better Tuesday and thought she ought to go to work. But by noon she was exhausted, and her wastebasket was filling fast with tissues.

"Do us all a favor and go home," Julie pleaded.

"But I've got so much to do."

"If you make us all sick, you'll have to do our work and yours next week. Go home." Julie swiveled her chair and called, "Chuck, tell Wynne to go home."

Chuck glanced up from his monitor. "You look like death warmed over. Go home."

She left without further protest and stopped on the way home for more juice and stronger cold pills.

When she turned in at her driveway, a splash of color on the front steps greeted her. She unfurled her umbrella and dashed for the entrance. A canning jar held several sprigs of light purple lilacs. A soggy sheet of paper was anchored by the jar, and she pulled it out.

"Wynne, I had to go to town and stopped to see if you were still sick. Grammy's lilacs are starting to bloom, even in this awful weather, and they should be just right for Memorial Day. Andrew."

She held the blossoms to her nose, but she couldn't smell the fragrance she knew was there. Ducking through the doorway, she sighed in relief to get out of the rain. After turning up the thermostat, she carried the jar into her bedroom and set it on her nightstand, took more medicine, and lay down.

Had Irene ordered Andrew to stop and check on her? And whose idea was it to pick the lilacs for her? She wanted to think the gesture was all Andrew's, but her brain was so muddled, nothing made sense.

She tried to think rationally about all the times she had seen Andrew, to reconcile his aloofness with the flowers and the achy longing that assailed her. As she drifted off to sleep, a fragmented memory of Wade zinged across her mind. She rolled over, telling herself that she could not, would not, love another man who was indifferent to her.

On Wednesday morning she felt better, but Chuck called her early.

"Sleep in this morning, and I'll have you cover a city council meeting tonight. Deedee is sick."

"Tonight? I have a regular thing I do on Wednesdays, Chuck. It's personal." She'd missed church on Sunday, and she'd set her heart on making it to the midweek Bible study.

"Are you well enough to work today?" Chuck asked.

"I think so."

"Then you come in at two and do the council meeting tonight. It comes with the job."

She was wide awake then, and she began to dress. The fragrant blooms on the bedside table caught her eye. She walked over and picked up the crumpled note and read it again. As she stared at the bold black letters, she knew it was too late.

She already loved his children and his grandparents, and Andrew was making a place for himself in her heart, whether he intended to or not.

"What's this?" Andrew stared down at the sheets of paper Thomas had placed in his hand. Lunch was over, and Irene was bringing the cookie jar to the table.

"You can read." Thomas poured milk into his glass and Andy's, then reached for a cookie.

Andrew scowled. He could see that he was holding the deed to the farm, but his grandfather was deliberately being cryptic. He glanced at Irene, but she was placidly removing Hallee's plate and silverware. He quickly skimmed the document.

"I don't get it."

"Your grandmother and I have decided to give you a gift."

Andrew clenched his teeth and flipped the page, staring at the last part of the text. "This is what you did yesterday, when you went off on that mystery ride?"

"That's right, son. The farm is yours now."

Andrew made himself take two deep breaths before replying. "I don't want the farm."

Irene smiled at him. "That's what we were hoping you'd say."

"Then why did you sign it over to me?"

Thomas took a long swallow of milk. "Well,

see, this way, you can decide what to do with it, and you can take your time. Irene and I will just keep on the way we are, but your future and the twins' is in your own hands now."

"We're retiring." Irene smiled as she took away Andy's dishes. "You know the doctor said your grandpa needs to retire."

Andrew took another deep breath, looking up at the ceiling. "What am I supposed to do? Help me out here. Do you want to go on living here while I keep the dairy operation running, or do you want to go to a retirement inn, or am I supposed to find you a little ranch house in a development? What do you want?"

Thomas shook his head. "No, son. What do *you* want? Just take your time and think about it. You've got the Bradley boy helping you now. That's a temporary thing, for the summer at most. If you want to keep farming on the scale we've been doing, you'll need to take Will Boyer on full time. If you don't want that, well, then, it's time to start considering alternatives."

Andrew pushed his chair back in exasperation. "Grandpa, don't do this to me."

"Do what?"

"I can't make all the decisions for you and Gram. What if I do the wrong thing?"

Hallee and Andy were staring, their eyes going from their father to Thomas, and back again.

His grandmother came and placed her hand on

Andrew's shoulder. "Grandpa and I have agreed, we need for you to handle things financially now. We'll give you our advice if you want it, but we did this to make it permanent. If anything happens to us, the property is yours outright."

A helpless fear formed in Andrew's stomach. "The doctor said Grandpa's healthy for a man his age."

Thomas chuckled. "The key phrase being, *a man my age*. I'm tired. Can't you just do this for me, son?"

"I guess so." Andrew swallowed, doubting his own words. "You've been taking care of me and the kids for a long time now. If you tell me what you want, I'll do my best to take care of you."

Irene squeezed his shoulder. "That's what we need. And we want to be with you. But we wanted this place to be yours. Or if you sell it, the money is yours. We know you'll do right by us."

"I will. Whatever you want." He still felt stricken. Everything had altered in less than a minute. His hearty grandfather suddenly looked old and frail, and Grandma bore an air of weariness he'd never noticed before.

Thomas laughed. "Let's not rush into anything."

Hallee rushed around the table and threw her arms around him. "You're not old, Grandpa!"

He chuckled and kissed her cheek. "I intend to enjoy a good many years yet with my family."

"Me, too," young Andy said solemnly.

Chapter 13

By Sunday morning, Wynne was feeling isolated and spiritually starved. She rose eagerly, free to point her car in the direction she most wanted to go. She arrived early at the church and greeted the Fortiers when they came and unlocked the door.

The Cooks came in just before Sunday school started, and she didn't have a chance to talk to them until the break between services. Irene went to her and held out her arms, and Wynne fell into them.

"We missed you so much," Irene cried.

"We were worried because you was sick," Hallee added.

"Worrying doesn't do any good," Thomas told her. He turned to Wynne. "We did a lot of praying for you this week, young lady."

"Thank you. I felt awful for a few days, but I'm much better now."

"Are you coming to our house today?" Andy asked.

"You bet I am." She felt happier than she had for a long time.

"Can I sit beside you in church?" Andy's face was eager.

"No, I want to," cried Hallee.

"Well, I think I'd like to sit between you," Wynne said. They settled down together in the row with Thomas and Irene, and Andrew sat on the end beyond Andy. He looked at Wynne over the boy's head, and although he hadn't said a word to her, his smile warmed her. She was glad Andy was sitting between them. Sitting next to Andrew would be far too distracting.

"Did you get the garden in?" she asked Thomas at lunch. The scent of Irene's oven-fried chicken, along with baked potatoes, green beans, and homemade biscuits, made Wynne feel hungrier than she had in weeks.

"We're going to have to replant a lot of the corn. It was so wet last week, I think most of the seed rotted."

"That's too bad. I'm sorry you have to work so hard." She looked over at Hallee. "The little calves must be all grown up by now."

Hallee had a mouthful, and her great-grandfather answered for her.

"Well, we've got a couple of new ones since you've been here, but I don't expect any more for a while." Thomas placed a large piece of chicken on her plate. "Do you have tomorrow off for Memorial Day?"

"Yes, we've done all the pages ahead that we could for Tuesday's paper, and just a few people are working tomorrow to cover the breaking news."

Irene leaned forward, her eyes glowing with mystery. "The family has planned something special, and we want you to come."

Wynne smiled. "I'd like that a lot. Does it involve flags and trombones?"

"And majorettes and flowers and a firing squad," Thomas admitted, laughing.

"We don't have a cannon," Andrew said regretfully, "but we'll have a picnic here after it's over."

"Are you doing this for me?" Wynne asked.

"Yes," Andrew replied.

His answer astonished her, but Thomas chimed in with a gentle correction.

"For all of us."

Andrew arched his eyebrows. "What about your sister and her husband? Are they doing anything special?"

"I'm sure they'll be spending the day with Rob's family. They'd include me, but this picnic you mentioned sounds interesting."

"Call Rebecca and tell her you have other plans," Thomas said.

"I believe I will."

After lunch, Wynne prepared as usual to help Irene with the dishes, but her hostess forbade her to enter the kitchen again.

"You are going to sit down in the living room.

Hallee and Andy are my helpers today. You go and sit. Thomas and Andrew can show you the picture albums."

"I've been wanting to see them," Wynne admitted, "but I'm capable of helping you first."

"No, that's the way it's going to be today," Irene insisted.

Thomas drew her into the living room, and Andrew followed silently. He took a seat in an armchair, and Thomas sat down beside Wynne on the sofa, picking up a photo album Irene had laid out on the pine coffee table.

"This one is sort of a family tree album that Irene made for me. She said we needed an album with all the presidents in order."

"All the presidents?" Wynne asked in confusion.

"Yes, all of us Cook men." Thomas's eyes twinkled. "I call this the Cook Book."

She chuckled.

"Of course, when my great-nephew Tyler married Amelia Page, we had to add a Page to the Cook Book."

Wynne exploded in laughter.

Andrew smiled indulgently. "Grandpa's been telling that joke since Tyler and Amelia got married eleven years ago."

"Well, now." Thomas opened the cover to the first photograph. "This is my own father, George

Washington Cook. He's the one who started it all."

"George Washington Cook," Wynne repeated, a smile playing at her lips.

"Yes. You see, when my father was a handsome young fellow, he met a lovely lady named Martha Niles. George and Martha, don't you see? There she is, my mother." He pointed to an old photograph on the next page.

"Oh, she's lovely." Wynne studied the face, but she couldn't see that Thomas resembled her. He definitely looked more like his father.

"Yes, and they had a fine family. Two boys and two girls. This is the oldest, my brother, John Adams Cook. That's me as a whipper-snapper."

"Thomas Jefferson Cook," Wynne read from beneath the picture of the young Thomas, with his twinkling eyes. Even with his full head of brown hair, she couldn't mistake him for anyone else. "I think I'm beginning to understand."

"You're catching on? Because my two sisters are named Abigail and Dolly."

Her grin widened. "I think I like your father."

"Well, that was just the beginning." Thomas turned the page. "John got married in 1964, and he had a son the next year. He and his wife decided to continue the tradition and named their boy James Madison Cook. Then we had our oldest, Jim." He paused, looking expectantly at Wynne.

"Don't tell me. James Monroe Cook."

"That's right. Then John and Jenny had another boy, and they named him John Quincy Cook. We call him Jack."

"And then you had Andrew," Wynne supplied.

"No, first we had Rachel. We named her for Mrs. Jackson. Then Andrew Jackson came along, followed by Martin Van Buren and William Harrison."

"My uncles, Marty and Bill," Andrew put in.

"Did your sisters name their children for presidents?" Wynne asked.

"No, it's only those with the Cook name," Thomas said. "The next generation thought it was an interesting thing, so James, my brother John's son, named his boys John Tyler, who goes by Tyler, James Polk, and Millard Fillmore. Then Jack had a boy and named him Zachary Taylor. My oldest boy, Jim, had the next two sons, and he named them Franklin Pierce and James Buchanan. We call that James "Bucky." Then Jack had another boy. That's Abe Lincoln." He had turned the pages as he talked, pointing out each "president" to Wynne.

"He ought to have a beard." Wynne scrutinized the picture of a stocky, blond young man. "They actually named him Abraham Lincoln Cook?"

"Had to. The tradition was strong by then."

"He didn't *have* to," said Andrew. "He just did. Then it was my Daddy's turn."

"Oh," Wynne gasped. "Andrew Johnson!"

"It worked out just right," Andrew agreed. "And it means I'm not quite a junior."

Wynne smiled in delight. "Then what?"

Andrew frowned in concentration. "Well, somehow I got a sister, Phoebe, in there, and then Uncle Marty and Aunt Sarah had Ulysses Grant. He goes by Grant. But when Aunt Sarah was expecting again, Uncle Marty said if it was a boy, he wasn't going to name him Rutherford Hayes, no matter what. He hated the name."

"So, what happened?"

"He circumvented the tradition," Thomas said solemnly.

"Was it a girl?"

"Oh, no, it was a boy, but Marty refused to name the little tike Rutherford. So he skipped right over Hayes and went to James Garfield. Then my Andrew had another boy, and he named him—"

"Wait." Wynne held out her hand to stop him. She looked at Andrew. "Let's see. Your brother's name is Chet, so I guess your father didn't like Rutherford, either."

"That's right," said Thomas. "He went right on to Chester Arthur. Bill didn't have any boys, just a passel of girls, so there we were with no Rutherford Hayes Cook. It was kind of sad, like someone in the family was missing. Some people who knew about the presidents thought there must have been a baby Rutherford that died."

"So the tradition ended with that generation?" Wynne asked.

"No, not quite. You see, Marty and Sarah had another child. A girl this time. Guess what they named her."

"I have no idea."

Thomas said slowly, "Ruth—Ford—Cook. Get it?"

A smile spread all over Wynne's face. She turned to Andrew. "Is he telling the truth?"

"Yes, it's my cousin Ruth. So then cousin Tyler decided to keep it going. He was the first one in my generation to have a son—well, two, actually—and he named them Grover Cleveland and Benjamin Harrison. Then Millard had William McKinley, and Frank had Theodore Roosevelt—T.R. we call him."

Thomas turned the album pages to keep up with Andrew's narrative.

"Let's see, William Taft must be next." Wynne could see the Cook resemblance in the smiling, blond children.

"Yes, that's Abe's only son," Andrew said. "So far, anyway. Billy's six, and he's a little dickens."

"He's a handful," Thomas agreed. "Then there was Frank's middle boy, Woody, for Woodrow Wilson."

"Then it was my turn," Andrew said darkly.

200

"This family will never forgive me for naming Andy after my father."

Wynne stared at him. "That's amazing. How did you dare?"

"Well, it was a crazy time. Joyce and I had talked about it, and we knew she was having twins. If they were both boys, we'd have had to name them Warren and Calvin, and she didn't like those names. We'd been in Germany for a while, and we decided that, since there wasn't any family around telling us what we had to name them, we'd just pick whatever names we wanted."

"Andrew always had a rebellious streak," Thomas said.

Andrew shrugged. "In the end we decided to name them for our fathers if they were both boys. Andrew and Robert. Well, I ended up with one boy and one girl. The German officials were after me to sign the birth certificates, so I picked Andrew Jackson the second, after my father, and Hallee for the little girl. Joyce had picked that name, and I wanted to . . ." His voice trailed off.

"But that's still not the end of it," Thomas said cheerfully. "We all forgave Andrew, under the circumstances, and three years later his brother Chester presented us with Warren Harding Cook. His cousin Frank already had two boys with presidential names, so when he had another last year, he named him Calvin." He triumphantly turned to a photo of a laughing, fat baby. "And this is the latest addition to the Cook Book, Grant's son, Herbert Hoover Cook. They call him Bertie."

"I am overwhelmed," said Wynne.

Thomas smiled. "We're all hoping Franklin Pierce has another son, so he can name him Franklin Roosevelt."

"Or Franklin Delano Cook," Andrew said.

Wynne shook her head. "I knew this family was special, but I had no idea how special."

"Bull headed," Andrew corrected. "Come on outside and see the new calves."

Wynne leaned over and kissed Thomas's cheek.

"Thank you for the history lesson. I enjoyed it tremendously. Are you coming with us?"

"No, I think not." He smiled and took the album to the bookcase.

Wynne followed Andrew through the kitchen, where Andy and Hallee were putting away the silverware.

"Where you going?" Hallee cried.

"Out to see the calves." Andrew pinched her nose gently.

"I wanna come," shouted Andy.

"You finish helping Grammy, then you can come out."

Irene smiled. "We've still got some pans to scrub."

Andrew opened the screen door, and Wynne

walked slowly with him toward the barn. A few butterflies kicked up in her stomach. He was voluntarily spending time with her. She hadn't been prepared for the change in his attitude, but there was no denying it. Instead of leaving her alone with his grandparents, he'd stayed around and been cordial. And now he seemed to actually want to talk to her alone. Wynne's pulse quickened as he turned away from the milk room door and headed around the corner of the barn.

"Out here."

"You've got all the babies outside now?"

"Yup. We're even putting the milkers out days now. There's enough grass."

They strolled around the corner of the barn toward the hutches. Wynne spotted the two newest Jersey heifer calves, lying in the sun in their wire pens.

"They're so tiny! What are their names?"

Andrew eyed her warily. "Wynne and Lose. Blame the kids."

She laughed.

"We call Lose 'Lucy,' though."

"That's much better."

Andrew opened the wire gate on the first enclosure and coaxed the little calf over to the fence so Wynne could pet her namesake. She laughed as the bossy licked her hand.

"Come sit for a minute. We can wait for the kids to come out." Andrew led her to an empty hay wagon and sat on the open front. Wynne jumped up beside him and smoothed her skirt.

"My grandfather says he's retiring." He picked up a piece of hay from the floor of the wagon and stuck the stem in his mouth.

Wynne watched him intently. "What does that mean for you and the twins?"

He gazed out at the herd grazing contentedly along the green slope. "I'm not sure yet."

She nodded. "You'll have some decisions to make."

"Big ones. I think . . . we'll probably sell the farm."

She fought back the protest that sprang automatically to her lips and looked slowly around the barnyard. Already she loved this place. It must be agony to Andrew and the children to think of leaving the only home they had ever known.

"Grandpa and Gram have wanted to sell it for a long time. They were thinking of it before I came back from Germany. They really kept it to help support me and the twins."

"But you've helped them a lot."

"Sure. I don't think they could have kept it going by themselves. But now . . . it's time, you know?"

Wynne drew in a slow breath. "What will you do?"

He leaned back against the upright support of

the wagon side. "Guess I'll start looking for a job."

"Wow."

"Yeah, it's kind of scary. I never did that before."

"Have you told the kids?"

"Not yet."

The screen door slammed, and the twins came whooping around the corner of the barn.

"Hey," Andrew cried, scooping Hallee into his arms as she launched herself toward him. "You forgot something, pumpkin. Gotta have that helmet."

"Aw, it's too hot!"

"I know, but you've got a couple more weeks before you get checked out." He set her carefully down on the ground. "Go get it."

Hallee stalked sulkily toward the house, and Andy began climbing the inside of the wagon rack. Andrew frowned as he watched him. "Don't go over the top."

"Would he?" Wynne asked, watching the little boy uneasily.

"He did it yesterday. Climbed down the outside. It scared me, I'll tell you, after Hallee's little episode."

She couldn't help smiling a little.

When Andrew smiled back, she felt a rush of joy. Perhaps he wouldn't be her antagonist, after all.

"Tell me something." His gray-blue eyes had gone sober again. "You said you like working for the paper."

She grimaced. "I don't think that's exactly what I said."

He sat quiet for a moment, then shrugged. "All right, maybe it's not. I guess it doesn't matter what you said. Tell me what you meant."

Wynne slid off the end of the wagon and walked toward the nearest calf pen. She put her hands on the wire, and stood looking at little Wynne, the heifer.

"I like writing. I like meeting people. I used to be scared stiff to interview strangers, but I've gotten used to that. But there are some things about the job that I hate."

"Like what?"

She jumped. Andrew was standing very close behind her. She turned around and was uncomfortable with only four inches of country air separating them.

"Could we walk?" she asked.

"Sure. Let's go down to the stream." He led her toward a path that went down a slope toward maple and poplar trees. The red maple seeds were being replaced by small chartreuse leaflets. Wynne heard running water from somewhere below the tree line. Andy came racing from behind and ran on past them, toward the stream.

"Daddy, wait!"

They turned to see Hallee puffing toward them, wearing the despised helmet. As she reached him, Andrew squatted and swung her up on his shoulders. "Now, hang on." He kept his hands on her ankles and walked along beside Wynne.

She tried to sort out the components of her job that made her uncomfortable. "Some things at work just aren't any fun, but I can live with those. I can't choose my assignments, and usually that's all right. Somebody's got to do the boring stuff. But sometimes . . ." She looked up at him cautiously. "Sometimes I really wish I'd picked another profession."

They had reached the bank of a rushing stream, ten feet wide. Andrew swung Hallee to the ground. Andy already had his sneakers and socks off and was wading in the brook.

"Can I wade, Daddy?" Hallee asked.

"Yes, just be careful, and don't get your shoes wet."

The little girl sat down and pulled off her shoes and socks, setting them carefully on a rock.

"We can sit over here." He took Wynne to one side of the path and climbed up on a large rock that overlooked the stream. He held out his hand, and when she grasped it, he lifted her up beside him. She sat down, smoothing her skirt, very conscious of his proximity.

Andy and Hallee were up to their knees in the

water below them, stooping often to pick up stones from the bottom.

"So, basically the job is okay," Andrew prompted.

"Yes. I like writing, although it's hard some-times. I've made one friend there, Julie. Some of the others are hard to work with. Their values aren't the same as mine."

He nodded. "You always wanted to be a reporter?"

"No, not really."

"Then why did you?"

"Because I could."

His eyebrows puckered, but he said nothing.

"I guess I could have done a lot of things, but I changed majors part way through college, and since I liked to write, journalism seemed a logical choice. I figured it was a marketable skill." Wynne pulled her knees up under her full skirt and wrapped her arms around them.

"You wanted to be something else?"

"Yes. I thought I did, anyway."

"What?"

"An engineer."

He laughed, then sobered quickly. "Sorry. I'm not laughing at you. Well, not exactly."

"It's all right." She smiled and looked down to where Andy was pulling a big branch into the water and Hallee was filling her pockets with wet pebbles. Choosing a college major so she could be closer to a young man she admired. She deserved to be laughed at. Of course, she wouldn't tell Andrew about that.

"You could be an engineer, I guess." Andrew stretched out on the rock. "I didn't expect that, though."

"No, I couldn't. I have absolutely no aptitude for it. I didn't realize what it entailed at first, and I'm horrible at math. It was a foolish mistake on my part."

"Something tells me you don't usually make foolish mistakes."

She wavered for an instant between honesty and courtesy, and decided to get the issue out into the open. "I figured you thought I made nothing but."

His long lashes swept down over his eyes for an instant. He sat up straighter and faced her apologetically. "I didn't mean to insult you or hurt your feelings, Wynne, but it's true I've wondered at your choice of careers."

"I chose badly the first time. Maybe I didn't do any better the second." The camaraderie was gone, and she shivered.

"So, you decided you weren't cut out to design bridges, and you switched to journalism."

"There was a little more to it than that."

"Would you tell me about it?"

She sat still, wondering if it would be wise to open her heart to him. She wasn't sure she could trust him yet with the parts of her life that were still painful. She could see the futility now of her pining for Wade, but she didn't need to have someone else tell her she'd been foolish, especially Andrew. Talking about her lack of judgment might jeopardize the fragile friendship they were forming, and she didn't want to move backward now. "It's sort of personal."

Andrew watched the twins splashing below them, but his expression was thoughtful.

"Sometimes God uses things in a different way than we expected," he offered at last.

"How do you mean?"

"Even though there are some things you don't like about your job, you're good at it. The writing part comes easy for you. Very few people have that gift, and God can use that."

She was startled by his praise. Looking up at him, she caught her breath. His intense gray-blue eyes probed her silence. "Thank you."

As he sat quietly beside her, with one knee pulled up and his arm resting on it, she knew she didn't need to tell him her embarrassments. He understood her reserve and respected it, and he knew that she was putting some things in order inside. He was going through the same process, with issues in his own life. It struck her forcefully that, as different as they were, they had much in common.

He reached over and took her hand, holding

it gently, and Wynne caught her breath. It was totally unexpected, and her emotions ran riot as she tried to read his sober face.

"Something happened a long time ago," he said quietly. "When my dad died."

She nodded, waiting.

"I guess I've been prejudiced ever since, thinking reporters are all bad. I'm trying to deal with that. See, I've had some trouble separating what you do from who you are."

He glanced up suddenly, and she followed his gaze. High overhead, a jet crossed the sky, trailing a white path across the blue expanse, and she heard the faint rumble that had alerted him.

"I don't think God gave you a love of flying for nothing," she whispered.

His eyes widened in surprise.

"You're a good pilot," she added.

"I'm not that good."

"You told me you were going to be a flight instructor."

He avoided her direct gaze, but a hint of a smile tugged at his lips. "Okay, I'm good." He looked up again. The jet had disappeared beyond the branches of the trees, leaving its widening plume behind to slowly disperse. He sighed deeply and settled down on the rock, his shoulder touching hers, their fingers loosely twined.

She watched the children in silence, wishing the afternoon could last forever. It was so tranquil.

The sun, the water, the trees, the children's laughter, and an occasional lowing from far up the path. Wynne's heart pounded violently, and she didn't dare to move, for fear something would change.

Chapter 14

Wynne woke full of expectations on Memorial Day. She dressed in her denim jumper and a red T-shirt and went early to the farm. Andrew was still in the barn milking with the two hired men when Irene opened the kitchen door to her.

"I brought some holiday cookies." Wynne held out a plastic box.

Irene opened the container and peeked inside. Wynne's sugar cookies were stars frosted in blue and white, and rectangles with stripes of red and white.

"How clever!"

"I got inspired last night," Wynne said. "My mother used to do it for me. Of course, today's not my birthday, but we always celebrated on Memorial Day, whether it hit the thirtieth or not."

Irene gave her a quick hug. "You'll miss your family today."

"I saw my sister yesterday—that's where I was last night."

"Andrew told us where you were off to."

Wynne nodded. "We may see them today at the cemetery. Oh, and my mom and dad sent me a big box. It was on my front step when I got home Friday night."

"What was in it?" Irene looked almost as eager as Wynne felt.

"This, for one thing." Wynne held up a package of balloons. "Would you mind if Andy and Hallee and I blew them up later?"

"They'll love it. Just show them how to do it safely. What else did you get?"

"A blouse, a book, some stationery, and a stuffed cow."

"A stuffed cow?"

"Yes, I've told everyone about the farm, and my sister gave me the cow. It's a Holstein, though."

Irene laughed. "She didn't want to wait until Saturday and give it to you on the real day?"

"Well, I wasn't sure if I could be with them Saturday, and she was very excited about the cow. Almost like Hallee gets when there's a secret."

"I can only imagine." Irene took a cabbage and a bag of carrots from the refrigerator. "I'm going to make a coleslaw for the picnic."

Andy came pounding down the stairs and into the kitchen. "Grammy, hurry! Miss Harding's coming today." He stopped short when he saw Wynne and looked down at his sneakers. "Hi."

Wynne grinned. "Good morning!"

"Your shirt is inside out, Andrew Jackson," Irene scolded.

Andy turned his back and peeled off the T-shirt.

"Now, is that polite in front of ladies?" His great-grandma shook her head.

He stepped into the dining room and returned a few seconds later with his shirt on right side out, but backward.

Irene sighed, rummaging in her utensil drawer for the grater. "Now the words are on the back."

Wynne reached out to him with a smile. "Come here. Pull your arms in, and I'll help you."

Andy slid his arms inside the shirt, and Wynne tugged it around until "Fryeburg Fair" was on the front. "There you go."

He popped his arms back out through the sleeves and ran to the cupboard for a cereal bowl.

Thomas came in through the back door in his overalls, carrying a jug of milk.

"You're bright and early, missy."

"Couldn't wait any longer," Wynne said. "Hey, I thought you were banned from the barn."

"Just went out to get a little milk from the tank for breakfast."

Hallee came yawning into the kitchen, and Wynne got her a bowl and poured milk on her cereal. She helped Irene with her lunch preparations, and Thomas disappeared. At last Andrew came in from the barn, filthy from his morning chores.

"Better get washed up and changed," Irene told him. "The parade is at ten, and we want to get a good spot."

"What, I can't go like this?" Andrew winked at Wynne.

Irene surveyed him critically. "You smell like the barn, and you look like you slept there."

Andrew laughed. "Guess I'd better get a shower, then."

"And don't walk across the living room rug in those boots!"

"All right, Gram." He sat down on a chair and pulled his barn boots off, then set them by the back door and went toward the stairs in his stocking feet.

At last everyone was ready. Irene hovered anxiously as Andrew loaded her bouquets of lilacs and tulips into the back of the car.

Thomas brought a couple of folding lawn chairs. "Andrew, you'll have to take your truck. We don't have room for everybody with all those posies in there."

"Sure, I'll take the twins."

Andy went to stand in front of his father. "I want to ride with Miss Harding."

"All right, I'll take Wynne and Andy," Andrew said.

Hallee's face skewed in outrage. "Me, too!"

"You can come in the truck on the way home," Andrew told her. "Now, don't fuss about it."

Wynne shot Irene a worried glance, but Irene smiled happily and herded Hallee into the rear seat of the car. They drove two miles to the cemetery, and Andrew kept up a running monologue, telling Wynne who owned each house along the way, and sometimes who had owned it when he was a child, and occasionally who had owned it before that.

"You've got your grandfather's knack for history," she told him.

"Well, I've heard the stories all my life." He pointed to an old white house with an ell attaching it to a large, weather-beaten barn. "That's where Barney Holt broke his neck. He was bringing out a sled of wood one winter and fell off. The oxen kept going right up to the barn and just stood there waiting to be unhitched. His wife saw the team standing out there, and she thought it was funny, so finally she went out and found Barney lying on the trail."

"When did this happen?" Wynne asked.

"Oh, eighty or ninety years ago."

She laughed. "You have memories from another era."

"Comes from living with my grandparents all my life, I guess. I don't know how many times Grandpa's told me about Barney Holt breaking his neck. When Chet and I used to climb around the beams in the barn, he'd say, 'You boys better get down or you'll break your necks, just like old Barney Holt.' "

"And now Andy and Hallee have that. It's a wonderful thing you've given them, Andrew. Not many children have the privilege of living with their great-grandparents."

He nodded. "I'm thankful. The kids will always remember the farm and the folks. I'm glad they're old enough for that." He glanced quickly at Andy, who was listening, wide-eyed, then at Wynne.

The twins don't know that everything is going to change, she reminded herself.

She spotted her brother-in-law's Audi parked beside the road.

"That's Rob's car. He and Rebecca must be right around here someplace."

Thomas pulled his car to the side of the road, and Andrew parked his truck behind it. They all walked slowly along the road beside the cemetery. It stretched for half a mile on one side, and a smaller part of the graveyard spilled over on the other side of the road. Irene, Thomas, and Andrew were greeted by friends as they ambled along.

"That's the oldest part of the cemetery." Thomas pointed to the right, where the stones were thin slate or granite uprights. A white building stood at the edge of the yard, and several people were sitting in chairs on the porch.

Andrew had carried the lawn chairs for his grandparents, and he settled them on the gravel at the edge of the road. Far away, Wynne heard brass instruments and the throb of a bass drum. Her pulse quickened as the sound came closer and she recognized the march "American Patrol."

"Hey, you!"

Wynne turned and gave a little squeal as her sister moved in for a bear hug.

"Thought we'd see you here," Rebecca said.

"We saw Rob's car, and we were looking for you."

"We'd gone to visit Tommy Wallace's grave with Rob's parents. They're over there." Rebecca pointed farther along the gathering.

Wynne grabbed Andrew's sleeve and pulled him forward. He had Andy up on his shoulders.

"This is Andrew Cook and Andy. This is my sister, Rebecca Wallace."

Andrew's eyes lit. "Rob's wife, eh?" He let go of one of Andy's feet to shake her hand.

"That's right. He's with his folks. I'm sure he'd love to see you later." Rebecca looked up at Andy. "You must be Andrew, Jr."

"No, ma'am," Andy said solemnly. "I'm Andrew Jackson Cook the second, after my grandpa. My daddy's Andrew Johnson Cook."

"Oh, yes, I heard about you family's prestigious naming procedure."

Andy frowned, studying her face. Andrew smiled and gave a little shrug, but Wynne felt her cheeks heat. Andrew must be thinking— correctly—that she told her sister just about everything.

Irene and Thomas were watching with smile-wreathed faces. Hallee squirmed between them, held firmly in place by a hand on each side.

Wynne couldn't help laughing. "Come here, Hallee. This is my sister that I've told you about."

"Are you Becca?" Hallee tumbled forward, and Wynne caught her so she wouldn't hit the ground. Andrew had reluctantly let her leave her helmet in the car, though technically she was supposed to wear it for a few more days.

"This is Hallee."

"I'm very pleased to meet you, Hallee Cook." Rebecca stooped and shook Hallee's hand. And you're right. My name is Rebecca, but you may call me Becca if you wish." She straightened.

"And these are Andrew's grandparents, Thomas and Irene Cook." Pride filled Wynne's voice as she introduced the people she'd come to love.

After greeting the older couple cordially, Rebecca glanced down the road. The vanguard of the parade was almost upon them.

"I'd better get back to Rob and the fam."

Wynne and the twins called goodbyes, and Andrew said, "See you later" as Rebecca scurried away along the front edge of the crowd.

The color guard marched past them, with the American flag and the blue Maine banner held high. The band broke into "Stars and Stripes Forever," and the majorettes paced on the pavement and tossed their batons high. Thomas and Irene stood up as the flags passed. A contingent of uniformed veterans moved slowly into the driveway in front of the white building, stopping near the granite veterans' monument.

Several elderly men were marching, and men her father's age who had served in Kuwait, followed by younger men who had been deployed to Saudi Arabia, Somalia, Bosnia, Iraq, or Afghanistan.

She glanced up at Andrew. He was watching the procession somberly, now holding Hallee high on his shoulders so she could see. Andy pulled at his arm, trying to climb higher, and Andrew lifted him and let Andy wrap his legs around his waist.

"You should be marching today," Wynne said softly.

Andrew shook his head. "I decided not to. Last year I did, and Hallee had nightmares after. She thought I was going away, I think."

The oldest of the veterans marched forward with a large wreath of flowers and laid it on the monument, and a senior from the local high school stepped forward to recite the Gettysburg Address. Wynne shivered, realizing he was no younger than Andrew had been when he put on his uniform ten years ago.

Andrew leaned down close to her ear. "My cousin Abe is reading it in Sidney this morning. They've had him do it the last three years, because of his name."

Two of the oldest veterans read the list of the town's men and women who had served in times of war, beginning with the Revolution, through the War of 1812, the Civil War, the Spanish American War, World Wars I and II, the Korean Conflict, Vietnam, The Gulf War, and conflicts right up to the present. It took a long time. Wynne listened to the names, hearing over and over some of the surnames of the town's oldest families.

Hallee got bored and wriggled until Andrew set her down and let her go to Irene.

The honor guard stepped crisply forward and fired their rifles to honor the dead. Andrew clapped his hands over Andy's ears as the volleys rang out, sharp and precise, and Thomas covered Hallee's.

The first trumpeter from the high school band stood by the monument, playing "Taps." From far at the back of the cemetery on the other side of the road, it was echoed mournfully by the girl who played second chair trumpet. The crowd stood silent until the last note faded.

The ceremony was over, and Thomas and Irene folded up their chairs. As they walked back to their vehicles, dozens of friends greeted them. Cars pulled away, and the school bus edged past to pick up the band members.

Rob and Rebecca trotted over to them as they loaded the chairs.

"Andrew, great to see you." Rob pumped Andrew's hand. "Mr. and Mrs. Cook." He smiled at Thomas and Irene. After establishing that he hadn't seen the twins for nearly two years, he marveled over their size.

"Growing right up," Thomas said proudly.

"They sure are."

"We'd better get over to your folks' house," Rebecca told Rob softly.

He nodded regretfully. "We'll have to get together sometime, Andrew. We don't live that far away."

"I know. It's the farm. And the kids. Seems like we're always busy."

"Bring the kids down to swim!" Rebecca cried. "They'd love it. Do you know where the house is?"

Rob gave Andrew detailed directions, and then he and Rebecca left, walking along the edge of the road toward their car.

"All set?" Thomas asked.

"Guess so." Andrew opened the passenger door of his pickup.

"We'll drive down to the lot," Thomas said. "And we've got Andy."

Hallee got into the truck with Wynne and Andrew.

"Grammy always puts flowers on my folks' graves and George and Martha's, and Grandpa's brother's." Andrew's truck rolled slowly down a gravel drive between the rows of headstones, following Thomas's car.

They all got out near a grove of pines, and Irene began arranging her flowers to her satisfaction.

"Let me show you some of the family plots." Thomas took Wynne's arm and drew her away. Andy and Hallee skipped along with them.

"Here's my parents." Thomas nodded at a pink granite stone, where a small flag in a brass holder showed that George had served his country.

"George Washington Cook, 1900-1972," Wynne read. "Martha Niles Cook, his wife."

"Yes, and Irene and I will have the one on this side. My brother John is over here."

It made Wynne a little sad just to think of it, but the fact of dying eventually didn't seem to bother Thomas.

They walked on, and he pointed out more monuments of his loved ones then took her down narrow paths to show her some of the older graves. "Now, this is where the Careltons are buried," he told her. "David Carelton was one of the first settlers in this town. I'm a direct descendant."

Andrew called to the twins, and Wynne watched them run back to him, following the path carefully.

"Should we go back?" she asked.

"Likely he wants to take them to their mother's grave," Thomas said gently.

Wynne turned and walked beside him, farther from Andrew and the children. A lump formed in her throat. She should have realized this pilgrimage would be a reminder of Andrew's sorrow.

"Care to cross the road?" Thomas asked, and Wynne knew he was being tactful. "The Wymans are over yonder, in the oldest part."

They crossed together, mindful of traffic. Thomas went straight to the correct row, though Wynne didn't see how he could remember where each grave lay among so many.

"Simeon Wyman," she read.

"He was here before the revolution. Came up from Massachusetts. That's his wife Thankful's stone, but it's weathered bad. The slate ones seem to have lasted best."

Wynne tried to read the verse carved below the name Thankful, but couldn't make it out.

Thomas came to her aid. "It says, 'She hath done what she could.' "

Wynne arched her eyebrows at him. "Is that a Bible verse?"

"It is. Their daughter, Sarah Wyman, married Joel Richardson. Now, Joel was a real character. Came walking up the Kennebec River with nothing but his axe and his gun. He built himself a farm in the wilderness, and married Sarah in 1776."

He showed her a few more stones, and they strolled back across the road and down the paths until Wynne saw Andrew, tall and lithe, but standing with his shoulders slumped and his head bowed, with the twins on either side of him.

Irene came toward them, smiling cheerfully. "There, I think we've made a nice addition to the Cooks' lots this time. They'll throw the flowers out when it's time to mow again, so I suppose I'd better come down Friday and take things away, but I like to know it's pretty here, where our loved ones are laid to rest. Not for the dead, but for the living that come here to visit."

"Speaking of which—" Thomas squinted at a car inching slowly down the next gravel lane toward Andrew. "—it looks like the Turners are here."

Wynne watched as the station wagon stopped and a middle-aged couple, a younger man and woman, and a toddler got out and greeted Andrew.

"Looks like the middle boy, Henry, and his wife came along," Thomas noted.

They waited a few minutes, admiring the bouquets Irene had arranged on the family graves. Then Thomas led them at a leisurely pace toward the Turner lot.

"Well, Thomas," Mr. Turner called genially. "Think we'll get a decent hay crop this year?"

Helen Turner smiled at Irene. Her white slacks and green silk blouse, with a green and gold necklace and matching earrings, looked elegant to Wynne. Despite her careful grooming, she sported a deep tan and looked as though she could work hard. "I see you made a bouquet for Joyce."

"Oh, we can take it away," Irene said graciously. "You've brought a lovely plant."

"No, don't take it. It's very bright and cheerful. I'll just let Andrew set this pot on one side, and your vase on the other." She stood looking down at the marker that read, "Joyce Turner Cook," and after a moment she sighed. "I do miss my girl." At that moment she seemed very tired and sad.

Wynne hovered behind Irene, not wanting to be noticed, and wondering if she could just duck behind Andrew's truck until the Turners left. But she would have to pass close to Thomas and Mr. Turner to do that, and she knew Thomas wouldn't let her go by him without making an introduction.

"Hallee looks so much like Joyce." Hallee's braids hung down just below her shoulders. Mrs. Turner picked one up and let it slide through her hand.

"Don't be sad, Nana." Hallee took her grandmother's hand. "We're going to have a picnic today."

"A picnic, child? I suppose it's warm enough." Mrs. Turner glanced questioningly at Irene.

"We thought we'd barbecue this noon, for the first time this year."

Andy came close and looked up solemnly

into Mrs. Turner's face. "It's Miss Harding's birthday."

Wynne felt the blood rush to her face as Helen's eyes fixed on her. She looked around quickly to gauge Andrew's distance. He had joined Thomas and Mr. Turner after placing the potted plant near the headstone and was talking with them and Henry and his wife. Should she explain about her holiday birthday that wasn't on the holiday every year?

"I don't think you've met my friend, Wynne Harding." Irene drew Wynne forward. "Wynne was born on May thirtieth, and her family celebrates her birthday on Memorial Day each year. Dear, this is our neighbor, Helen Turner."

"How do you do?" Helen looked Wynne up and down critically.

"Nice to meet you." Wynne was glad she had worn the jumper instead of jeans or shorts, but even so, she wondered if passing this inspection was possible.

Mrs. Turner's undisguised speculation made her skin prickle. Andrew had claimed she held a grudge against him for taking her daughter away. Now she might think she had something else to hold against him. Wynne wished she could wear a big sign that said, "I'm Not After Your Son-in-Law."

"Wynne works for the newspaper." The pride in Irene's voice made Wynne's blush deepen. "She wrote the article about our church a couple of weeks ago."

"Oh, yes, I saw it." Mrs. Turner opened her mouth as if to say more, then closed it.

"You gals ready to go home and eat?" Thomas asked.

"All set." Irene smiled at Helen. "Come see us when you have a chance."

The two families separated into their vehicles. Wynne felt the eyes of the Turners on her as she hesitated beside Thomas's car.

"Come on, Hallee," Andrew called. "It's your turn to ride with Wynne and me."

Wynne felt as though she had committed a breach of cemetery etiquette. Her eyes found Irene's and pleaded silently for forgiveness.

Irene understood. "It's all right, dear. Go along with Andrew."

She walked toward the pickup, where Andrew was hoisting Hallee into the middle of the seat. He tugged the little girl's seat belt tight then held the door for Wynne. She climbed in, then he closed it and went around to the driver's side.

Thomas drove slowly around the end of the row of gravestones and up the next lane, and Andrew followed. Mr. Turner had backed his car out the other driveway, and it was disappearing around a curve in the road when Andrew's truck rolled onto the pavement.

"I could have ridden with your grandparents." Wynne looked at him over Hallee's head.

Andrew glanced at her in surprise, then back at the road. "Did you want to?"

"Well, no, but . . . I didn't want it to be awkward."

"Awkward?"

"Mrs. Turner . . ." Wynne couldn't voice what she felt. How could she tell him she'd been viewed as an interloper intruding on the territory that should have belonged exclusively to the Turners' daughter?

Andrew was silent for a moment, and Hallee rolled up the long, dangling end of her seat belt.

"I'm sorry you got caught in the middle of this," Andrew said at last.

"Hey, Daddy, want some tape?" Hallee asked. She let the rolled seat belt go and said gleefully, "Sorry, all gone!" She began rolling it up again.

Wynne took a deep breath. "In time they'll realize I'm not . . ."

"We buried Joyce in their lot because they wanted it that way." Andrew drove with his eyes fixed on the road ahead. "They asked me if they could. At that point, I wasn't sure yet if I'd stay here or go back in the service. They said I could end up anywhere, and they wanted to know she was buried with their family, so I let them."

"Do you wish you hadn't?"

"No, it's all right." He adjusted the sun visor and threw her a glance. "I was feeling really guilty. I'd taken her away, and I didn't bring her back safe. I figured it was one small thing I could do to comfort them."

Wynne nodded.

"Miss Harding, want some tape?" Hallee asked cheerfully.

"Sure, I'd love some."

Hallee flipped the seat belt out and crowed, "Sorry, all gone!"

"Settle down, pumpkin," said Andrew.

Wynne smiled at Hallee. "You're sneaky."

"What rhymes with sneaky?" asked Hallee.

"Oh, brother," said Andrew.

"Squeaky?" asked Wynne.

"Leaky," said Hallee.

"How about creaky?" said Andrew.

Wynne smiled at him. "Or freaky."

"Look, it's been almost five years. Helen and Bob are the twins' grandparents, and they love them, but I don't think they really care what happens to me."

Wynne watched his tanned hands on the steering wheel as he turned in at the Cooks' driveway. Was he saying he didn't mind if people assumed they were a couple? Their relationship had changed from confrontational to tolerant to amicable. Now they seemed to be creeping toward a warmer stage, but the obstacles were many, and Wynne wondered if they could ever get past them.

"Irene made a point of introducing me as her friend."

His lips twitched as he stopped the truck and put the gearshift into park. "She'd go a long way to smooth things over for me. I'd say you're a friend of the entire Cook family by now, wouldn't you?"

"You're my friend." Hallee reached up to hug her, and Wynne hid her confusion as she returned the little girl's embrace.

Chapter 15

Wynne was soon helping Irene set the picnic table with paper plates and bowls of salad and chips. Andrew manned the grill, and Thomas was almost as excited as the twins, as they blew up the balloons from Wynne's birthday box. He tied them to the rustic table with lengths of string. A light breeze came up, stirring their hair and waving the balloons as they ate their hamburgers.

It's like a complete family, Wynne thought, looking around the table at the grandparents and the children, and Andrew, solid and strong beside her. She wished very much that it was her family.

Andrew caught her glance and smiled. "I guess your family's having a picnic about now."

"Probably. I should call them tonight."

Irene rose and picked up the meat platter. "I'll bring out the dessert. Hallee, you come help me."

"Happy almost birthday, m'dear," said Thomas.

"Oh, thank you. It's been a very nice almost birthday so far."

"Did we duplicate your usual festivities?" he asked.

"It was quite different, but the same, if that makes sense. I always feel so patriotic on my birthday. And this town puts on a nice ceremony."

"Don't we?" said Thomas. "We do the Fourth

233

of July up even bigger. Much bigger parade, and games and exhibits and such."

Irene came in from the kitchen carrying a cake with twenty-three candles ablaze. Hallee followed her, carrying Wynne's plastic box of cookies.

When the cake was safely on the table, Wynne stood to embrace Irene. "You shouldn't have!"

Irene squeezed her. "Nonsense. It was fun."

Thomas began to sing "Happy Birthday," and the rest joined him. Wynne sat smiling and blushing until they had finished.

"Make a wish," Thomas reminded her.

"Do you believe wishes come true?" she asked, laughing.

"If you wish for God's will."

"You can't catch him," said Irene.

Wynne chuckled. "I'm ready. Here goes." She closed her eyes for a moment. *I wish this was my family.* Could that possibly fall within the parameters of God's will? She gulped in air and made her breath last until every candle was out.

"Hooray!" Hallee hugged her exuberantly, and Andy grinned.

"Good job! You get your wish."

"I hope so, Andy."

"Oh, Andrew, the ice cream is in the refrigerator freezer," Irene said. "Would you . . . ?"

He got up quickly and went to the house.

When he came back, he had a carton of

234

vanilla ice cream and a gaily wrapped package.

"What's this?" Wynne asked warily, as he placed the gift before her.

"Nothing much," said Irene. "Just something we put together for you."

Wynne carefully lifted the Scotch tape and laid back the wrapping paper. She opened the box to reveal a fluffy brown teddy bear with an Uncle Sam hat and a white vest sprinkled with red and blue stars. In his paw was a small American flag.

"Grammy made the hat and vest," Andrew told her.

"I love it! He's perfect."

"Seemed right for the holiday girl." Irene gave her a huge smile.

After the cake was cut and consumed, Andy asked, with wide eyes, "Daddy, can we go to the brook?"

"I guess so. Go put on some shorts."

Thomas stretched his arms. "Guess I'll take a nap."

"You do that." Irene began stacking the dishes, and Andrew helped strip the picnic table while he waited for the children. They came running out a few minutes later. Hallee had on pink shorts and a yellow tank top.

"Do I have to wear the helmet, Daddy?"

"What do you think?" Andrew carried the trash can to the kitchen door.

Irene followed him inside. "Go on. Get those children in the water. Wynne, you go, too."

"Oh, no, I'm on the dish crew today."

She stayed with Irene until every bit of leftover food was put away and the kitchen sparkled.

"Now, get."

Wynne laughed. "You're getting mighty bossy."

"Once you're past seventy-five, you're allowed." Irene shooed her toward the door.

Wynne walked slowly along the path, savoring her freedom from the office on such a glorious day. The maple leaves were unfolding and expanding in the sun, and the ferns near the stream were twice as tall as the last time she'd seen them.

Andrew had rolled up his jeans and was ankle-deep in the water, helping Andy with his primitive dam. He had allowed Hallee to remove her helmet and sit quietly in the shallows. Wynne thought the water was a little lower than it had been the week before.

"Miss Harding!" Hallee wriggled with joy, and Wynne sat down on the grass near her and slipped off her sandals.

Andrew looked up and gave her a crooked smile. "We could use an engineer here."

"Don't look at me. But I could write a story about it." Wynne lowered her feet into the cool water.

Hallee leaned toward her and pinched her big

toe. "Watch out, Miss Harding! A crab will get you."

"You can't fool me. There aren't any crabs in this brook."

Hallee giggled.

"Get some more sticks, Andy. We'll pack it with mud on the upstream side." Andrew was immersed in the construction job, but he smiled wistfully as he worked with his son.

This is it for him, Wynne thought. The last Memorial Day here. The last summer on the farm. The last chance to play in the brook with the kids. He would never forget this day, but just to be certain, she took out her cell phone and snapped several pictures.

Chapter 16

It was hot for the middle of June, and Andrew removed his blazer before getting in the truck for the drive home. The pickup's air conditioning hadn't worked for two years, and he couldn't afford to fix it. He loosened the knot in his necktie and tossed it onto the seat with the jacket.

Pete Turner's pickup was in the barnyard when he got home. Pete and Thomas sat in lawn chairs in the shade of the silo, sipping lemonade. Andrew climbed slowly out of his truck and slung the jacket over his shoulder. He walked across the grass toward them, his necktie trailing from his other hand.

"You look beat." Thomas edged his chair farther into the shade, and Andrew sat down on the tongue of the hay wagon.

"Beat, but not defeated."

"Your grandpa says you're job hunting." Pete was definitely curious, and Andrew was sorry he didn't have anything positive to tell them.

"Looking and finding are two different things." Thomas heaved himself up out of his chair.

"Where you going, Gramp?"

"Just gonna get you a cold drink. You sit still. Give me your duds." Thomas took the jacket and tie and headed for the kitchen door.

Pete raised his eyebrows expectantly. "He says he'd be willing to discuss selling the property again, but he doesn't own it anymore."

Andrew scowled. "Yeah, well, that wasn't my idea."

"Still, if you're the owner . . . didn't I just hear that the owner is job hunting?"

"You're still interested, then?"

"I'd give my eye teeth for this place. You know that."

"Well, don't start pulling them out yet. I don't seem to have many marketable skills, as Miss Harding calls them."

"Miss—oh, the reporter. I heard about her. How's she mixed up in this?"

"She's not."

"You sure?"

Andrew moved over to Thomas's empty chair, avoiding looking directly at his friend. Pete knew him too well.

"She's a friend of the family, that's all."

"Hmm. Your kids were out here a few minutes ago, and Hallee couldn't stop yammering about Miss Harding."

"Hallee can't stop yammering for two seconds."

"I heard she's pretty."

Andrew threw his head back, staring up at the barn roof. Maybe he should tell Pete how mixed up he was inside, how exhilarated he felt in Wynne's presence, and how guilty that made him feel. Or maybe he should just keep quiet. His silence in itself would speak volumes. Pete would get the picture.

"Look, Andrew, we're not kids. If you've got your eye on a woman, that's great."

"The only thing I've got my eye on is getting a job that will support this family."

"Naturally." Pete looked skeptical. "What are you looking for?"

"Anything where the job description doesn't include *experienced milker*."

Pete nodded soberly. "I'll keep my ears open."

"We understand each other, then," Andrew said.

Pete stood up as Thomas came from the kitchen holding a dripping glass. "We'll see you Saturday, Tom."

"Right!" Thomas brought the lemonade to Andrew and sat down in the other chair as Pete's pickup pulled out. "He says they'll send a big crew over to help us get in the hay you cut yesterday."

"What about their hay?"

"They're caught up. Bob will stay and chop haylage, but the boys will come. Maybe Donna and Judy, too."

Andrew nodded and took a long drink.

"Donna's as good as a boy any day for haying," Thomas added. "So, how did the interview go?"

Andrew shook his head. "They've got a million applicants. I'm not cut out for that kind of work,

241

Grandpa. Sitting at a desk all day and trying not to offend people."

"Well, it was worth a try."

"I dunno."

"There's an ad in today's paper for a supervisor at a paper mill."

Andrew shook his head. "I don't know anything about making paper, Gramp. That's a specialized job."

"Don't give up yet."

"Oh, I'm not giving up. I just feel like I haven't come anywhere close to the right job."

"You will. The Lord's got something out there for you."

"I hope He tells that to the fellow at the job service soon." Andrew looked toward the pasture, where the cows were grazing placidly. "Did Will and Mike make out all right with the milking today?"

"They did fine."

Andrew stood up wearily. "Good. I'm going to take a shower before supper. Then I just want to sit with the kids for a while. I hate being away all day."

"Son, if you think it's better, you can keep this place. I didn't mean to pressure you. If you'd really rather keep on the way you have been—"

"No. We're not turning back. And Pete still wants the farm."

"He told me he was going to put money on a place in Readfield."

"That was before he heard we might sell."

Thomas's white eyebrows quirked. "You think he'll hold off making an offer on that other farm?"

"Yes. He's always had his eye on this one. I didn't come right out and say it, but he knows if I find a good job, I'll sell to him."

Thomas bit his upper lip. "Things will work out."

Andrew nodded. "One way or another."

"I guess I ought to tell you, we invited Wynne to come and help Saturday."

He stood silent for a moment, then gave a short laugh. "Why did you do that? You know she's not strong enough to be much help. I doubt she could lift a bale of hay if her life depended on it."

"She might surprise you."

Wynne's work had kept her busy for the last two weeks, keeping her away from the farm. Chuck Barnes had tried her patience more than once, changing her schedule at the last minute and dumping assignments on her that none of the more experienced reporters wanted to do.

On Thursday, she faced the stiffest test ever when Chuck called her to his desk.

"The Kennebec County Superior Court is picking a jury today and tomorrow. You be in

Augusta at eight Monday morning for the start of the trial."

"Not the Pushard murder trial?"

"Is there another one next week?"

Wynne gulped. "Chuck, I've never covered a trial before. Are you sure you want me on this?"

His eyes narrowed, and he sat looking up at her for a moment. "I'm sure. You did a good job on the Stratton case, and we got some favorable feedback on your style. Sensitive, caring writing is in vogue right now, especially when we're discussing crimes against women and children."

Her lower lip quivered. "I really don't want to do this one. That little girl. Chuck, I don't think I can sit through the testimony."

He sighed and leaned back in his chair, his long legs extending into the aisle beside her. "You're going to make me say it, aren't you?"

"What? That I don't have a choice?"

"No, that's obvious. I meant the G word." He leaned toward her conspiratorially. "You're good. Too cautious, but you're developing your own style. And, listen, if you tell Deedee or Clint I said that, I'll deny it."

Wynne pressed her lips together and fought back the revulsion that filled her. Why didn't the grudging praise from her difficult editor thrill her? She ought to be walking on air.

"This little pep talk is supposed to fire me up for the trial, isn't it?"

He shrugged. "I try to time my compliments strategically. It's part of management training."

"Chuck, please don't make me do it."

"Come on, it should be an easy week for you, maybe two. You sit all day in the courtroom in Augusta, and file one story a day. One front page story. It's a cushy assignment, Harding!"

She shook her head. "I don't want it. Send Deedee or Clint."

"Clint's too green."

Wynne couldn't argue with him. The young reporter they'd hired after Jim Dowdy left was fresh out of college in Iowa. Not only wasn't he used to the *Guardian*'s routines, but he was so obviously "from away" that people had a hard time opening up to him.

"I know you don't like the crime beat," Chuck said. "We've established that. But I need you on this one. Hallowell called me about this particular story. The public is in a lynching mood, and the publisher wants it handled with a soft touch. Nobody else could do it as sensitively as you. Deedee would make a circus out of it. As for Melanie, well, the thought of Melanie covering a murder trial makes me shudder."

"So that leaves me."

"If you prefer to think of it that way. In reality, you're the best reporter for this job."

"No."

His eyes widened. Wynne took a deep breath

and prayed that the tear suspended from her eyelashes wouldn't fall. Chuck's expression hardened.

"Maybe we should step into the conference room to finish this discussion."

Chapter 17

On Saturday, Wynne rose early and dressed in old, comfortable jeans and a short-sleeved lavender shirt. The forecast was for unrelieved heat. She braided her hair and grabbed a baseball cap, then drove to the farm. Wynne looked forward to a day of haying as a physical challenge and an emotional rest.

"Hi! The Turner boys will be over as soon as their milking is done," Irene said when she stepped into the kitchen. "Thomas and Andrew are already out baling."

"I hope Thomas won't overdo it." Wynne picked up a dish wiper and dried the frying pan Irene had scrubbed and rinsed.

Irene's smile was grim. "We'd have to hog tie him to keep him out of things today. At least he's driving, so he won't be trying to do much lifting. I admit I'll be glad when we get him away from here, so he can't always be trying to do too much."

"Do you have any idea where you'll move to?"

"Not yet. Andrew's starting to get discouraged. There don't seem to be any good jobs open for him here."

"It's only been a few weeks."

"I know, but he's finding it hard. He never had

to sell himself before. He's thinking about going to flight school to upgrade his pilot's license."

"I'm glad he's considering that. He loves it so much!"

Irene shook her head. "I don't know if it's a good thing or not. He'd have to move away. To Portland at least, maybe out of state."

"I didn't think of that." Wynne hung up her dishtowel and lined the edges up straight. "Would you and Thomas want to move away? You've always lived in this area."

"This is home." Irene sighed as she began to scrub the counter. "We're not sure we ought to uproot at our age. And it would be harder for Andrew to find a place big enough for all of us. Maybe we should just go into one of those retirement centers."

"The twins would take it so much easier if you were going to live with them."

"Maybe yes and maybe no." Irene's voice held a stubborn edge. "We old folks might end up being a burden to Andrew."

"Oh, Irene, don't talk like that. You let him be a burden to you when he needed you. He wants you with him. You know how much he loves you."

"Yes, he loves us." She eyed Wynne appraisingly. "But it's possible Thomas and I might be in the way."

"That's silly! It would be a tremendous relief to Andrew to have you along."

"Hmm." Irene looked out the window as the sound of a throbbing motor drew near. "If you insist on tossing hay bales, you'd better get out there. Henry's here, and Thomas just drove up with the first wagon."

Andrew hopped down from the wagon as Thomas parked it at the bottom of the hay elevator slanting up from the ground to the door of the mow high above. Wynne came out from the kitchen, pulling on Irene's worn work gloves. After one glance, Andrew ignored her. He knew he was being watched by many eyes, and he wasn't sure he could withstand the scrutiny if he let himself think about Wynne.

Thomas stayed in the tractor cab while Andrew and Will Boyer unhitched the wagon and pushed it into just the right position, blocking the wheels with short pieces of wood.

Pete had gone straight to the hayfield to drive the second tractor. Andrew could just see it inching along in the field across the road, pulling a green baler. Every half minute, the baler dropped a rectangular bale of hay on the ground behind it.

Pete's wife and his oldest son were sitting on a bale resting, but when Thomas got back with an empty wagon, Judy would take Pete's place in the tractor seat, pulling the baler. Thomas would drive along slowly, pulling the wagon, while Pete and Jordie loaded the bales and stacked them in neat tiers in the wagon.

Henry and Bob Junior had come to help with the unloading. Donna Turner, dressed in jeans and a yellow T-shirt, was ready to heave the bales from the wagon onto the elevator. As Wynne neared the wagon, she called, "Hi! I'm Donna. We met at the cemetery a few weeks ago."

Andrew deliberately stayed in the background and let Donna introduce Wynne to her husband, Henry, and his younger brother, Bob.

"All right, Will, do you want to stack in the loft with me?" Andrew asked.

"Sure thing," Will said.

"All right, then, I think we can keep up with the four of you down here." Andrew looked appraisingly at Wynne, Donna, Bob, and Henry.

Wynne stared in open amazement as Will hopped onto the elevator and climbed it, ladder-like, to the mow door above.

"Daddy, I want to go up with you," Andy cried.

Andrew hesitated. "Okay, but you can't climb the elevator. Come on, I'll take you up." As he walked toward the milk room door with Andy, he called over his shoulder, "Hallee, you stay down here."

"I wanna come," Hallee yelled.

He stopped and looked at her sternly. "Don't you try to come up there. You hear me?"

Hallee nodded miserably.

Wynne stepped toward her. "Hallee, you don't need your helmet anymore!"

Hallee's smile broke out. "No, my head is all better now."

"I'm so glad." Wynne looked toward Andrew, and he smiled at her gratefully. He turned away, and Henry's grin warned him that he was in for some ribbing.

When he reached the hay mow door, he saw that Thomas had put the tractor in gear and driven around the corner of the barn near the calf hutches, where another empty wagon was waiting for him to haul to the field.

"All set," he called to those below.

Henry flipped the switch that started the conveyor chain on the elevator, and he, Bob, and Donna each lifted a bale by the tight twine and set it carefully on the elevator. Prongs on the chain grabbed the hay, and the bales rose slowly up and up to the mow door, where Andrew and Will grabbed them and stacked them in dense rows.

Andrew looked over his shoulder at his son. "Andy, stay back, now. Keep out of the way."

"I can stack, Daddy."

"All right, but you start a stack over there by the wall, where nobody will step on you." Andrew heaved a bale close to the point he had indicated, so Andy could try to make his own haystack.

When he looked down at the wagon again, Wynne had climbed aboard and was lifting bales onto the elevator. She had some grit. Probably wouldn't last through the first wagon, though. Hallee was playing in the driveway, piling pebbles into tiny castle walls, and he was glad she had accepted the situation.

The four in the wagon developed a rhythm that allowed them to take turns positioning their bales without getting in each other's way. When they had emptied about a third of the wagon, Donna climbed up on the top tier and began tossing bales down to the three below.

Andrew steadily lifted each bale as it reached the top of the elevator and tossed it toward Will. Twice he threw one toward Andy, who pushed and tugged at the heavy bundles, determined to build his stack.

At last the wagon was empty, and Henry switched off the elevator. Bob climbed up the elevator and came in through the mow door to help them wrestle the last dozen bales onto the growing stacks. When they'd caught up, Andrew stood panting in the open doorway, the sweat streaming down his face and soaking his T-shirt. Bob joined him, hoping to catch a breeze.

"Let's get down there and get a drink," Bob said.

Andrew went to help Andy, who was struggling to get his last bale on top of the other two.

"Good workout." Will wiped his forehead with the back of his hand.

Andrew curled his lip. "You needed it, you lazy bum."

Will smiled. "Does Wynne know you're so ornery?"

Andrew threw him a sideways look as he pushed Andy's pile together. "Wynne is a friend of Irene's."

Will laughed. "I've heard that before."

Bob's eyebrows quirked. "Are we talking about that gorgeous girl in purple? Something I should know about?"

"Just a friend of Irene's," Will said with a wink.

Wynne sat down on the front of the wagon and took off her gloves.

"Got blisters?" Donna sat down beside her.

"Not yet. My hands are a little sore, though."

"Sign of a tenderfoot," Henry laughed.

"Don't tease her," Donna scolded, but she leaned against him when he came and sat beside her. "Wynne's not used to this, but she's got a lot of gumption."

"So, you and Andrew getting along pretty well?" Henry asked.

Wynne felt her face going scarlet. As if the exertion and the merciless sun weren't enough, she had to put up with teasing. "Well, we're friends, I guess."

"Hoo, yeah," Henry laughed. Donna elbowed him in the ribs.

"Lemonade!" Hallee shouted as Irene appeared in the kitchen doorway with a large pitcher and a package of paper cups.

"No, it's iced tea," Irene corrected. Donna hurried to help her. Wynne admonished herself for not moving faster, but her back ached as she stood up.

Irene appraised her. "You look as if you could use a cool drink, dear."

Wynne pushed back a strand of damp hair that had escaped her braid. "I'd like to jump in that pitcher."

Bob and Will balanced with their hands and feet on the side frames of the elevator and slid down to the wagon. Andrew and Andy came out of the milk room.

"Perfect timing." Andrew reached to take a paper cup from Donna just as Thomas drove into the barnyard with another full wagon.

"How many wagons do we unload?" Wynne asked.

"All of them." Andrew grinned at her, then relented. "Probably one more after that one."

"And you do this every day for how many weeks?"

"What, are you writing a story about haying now?" He reached out and tugged her braid gently, the way he often did Hallee's.

Wynne's heart lurched, but she stayed out-wardly calm and smiled at him. "Now, that's a thought. I'll bet they'd run a feature in the Sunday paper. I should have brought my camera."

Thomas glugged down a glass of tea. He left Judy Turner in the barnyard and drove back to the field to pull the last wagon around as Pete and Jordie stacked the bales in it. Andrew and his son went back up to the loft with Bob and Will, and the crew once again began to unload the seemingly endless stream of bales.

By the time the second wagon was empty, Wynne was sure she was crippled. Her hands throbbed where they had strained at the baling twine, and her back felt like it was permanently folded. She stretched her arms, then stood with her spine flat against the side of the wagon.

Andrew brought Andy down for a drink and a cookie. The third wagon, three quarters full, was already waiting for them.

Andrew's face was grimy, and rivulets of sweat had cut through the dirt. His wet hair was plastered to his brow, and his sweat-soaked T-shirt was caked with dust and hay chaff. In spite of the filth, Wynne felt her pulse accelerate when she caught him watching her. It went into high gear when he came to stand beside her.

"Tired?" he asked.

"I won't admit to that."

"You don't have to. It's all over your face."

"Like the dirt all over yours?" She smiled wearily.

"Guess so." He wiped his forehead with a grubby sleeve. "You'd better sit out this last one. Pete and Jordie will help."

"If Donna and Judy are helping, I'll help."

"Stubborn, aren't you? Donna and Judy are used to this." He looked over his shoulder toward where Will and Bob were sitting on the grass and then turned his back to them. He reached for her right hand and looked at the red, aching palm, then rubbed it gently with his thumb. "You don't have to prove anything," he said softly, looking into her eyes.

Wynne could barely meet his gaze. Her heart was hammering, and she wished suddenly that the haying crew was gone and she and Andrew were sitting on the rock by the cool stream.

She looked down at his strong fingers clasping her sore hand and received another jolt. A pale stripe of skin circled his finger where his wedding ring had been. Had he removed it because he was working with machinery today, or had he laid it aside for good?

"Irene said you might upgrade your pilot's license."

He shrugged. "Yeah, well, I haven't had much luck the last few weeks, looking for a job."

"Your grandfather would say luck doesn't exist."

He grimaced. "You got me. Listen, would you pray about this? We've got a buyer for the farm, but we don't have a place to go."

Wynne looked away from him, toward the pasture, catching her breath. "It's hard to think of this place without you. All of you," she added quickly. With the problems she was having at work, life here without the Cooks would be miserable.

"Well, I'd hate to move too far away. For one thing, Grammy's not too keen on it. And I just don't think I want to—" He looked around suddenly. "Where's Hallee?"

Wynne looked blankly toward the driveway, where she had last seen the little girl. "I don't know. She didn't come for a drink this time."

"Grammy," Andrew called sharply, dropping Wynne's hand, and Irene turned toward him. "Is Hallee in the house?"

"I don't think so. She—" Irene stopped suddenly and looked around. "I'll go check." She hurried to the back door.

Andrew looked around the barnyard uneasily. "Grandpa, will you go in and check the barn?"

Thomas handed his paper cup to Donna and went without a word.

"I'll go with you," Henry said.

Andrew looked up toward the mow door, then strode to the hay elevator and scaled it quickly. Wynne stood below, waiting, praying silently.

Irene came bustling from the house. "I don't think she's in there anywhere. I checked all the rooms and called to her."

Andrew appeared again at the mow door. "She's not up here. Any sign of her down there?"

They spread out over the yard, calling, "Hallee! Where are you, Hallee?"

Judy went with Irene back into the house to make a more thorough search.

Wynne glanced at Donna. "Sometimes the kids play at the brook down back."

"Let's go." Donna ran with her, around the corner of the barn and down the path toward the stream.

Wynne was relieved when they found no sign of Hallee near the brook. The water was scarcely four inches deep now, and she thought Hallee wouldn't be in danger there. Still, they walked along the bank a short way, calling to her, before turning dejectedly back toward the barn. A deep fear replaced Wynne's mild apprehension. As they approached the farmyard, they could hear the searchers still calling Hallee's name.

They came near the fence, and Wynne looked out over the sloping pasture, searching for a tiny form among the docile cattle that grazed, heads all pointed westward, flicking their tails at the flies.

"I don't see anything." Donna shaded her eyes

as she scanned the pasture. "Should we go down there to make sure?"

Seeing the little sheds nearby, Wynne said, "The hutches. Hallee loves to pet the calves."

They ran with renewed energy to the enclosures.

"Check this one," Wynne commanded. "I'll check the next one."

Donna opened the wire gate into Lucy's pen, and Wynne went on to the one where the little Jersey heifer that was her namesake dozed in the sun before its shelter. She looked toward the opening of the hutch and thought she saw a bundle lying just inside. Her pulse racing, she undid the gate and fastened it behind her so the calf wouldn't escape. It jumped up and shied away from her.

"Take it easy, Wynnie." She fell to her knees on the trampled turf. The limp form in the hutch was unmistakable. "Hallee! Hallee, honey, are you all right?"

She tugged at Hallee's ankle and gently pulled her out.

The little girl squirmed and moaned, then looked up at Wynne.

"Howdy, Miss Harding."

"Oh, you little scamp!" Wynne folded Hallee into her arms. "Donna! Donna, she's here."

Donna ran to the pen. "Really? You found her?" She stopped when she saw the little girl in overall shorts, filthy with mud and manure, cuddled in Wynne's arms.

"I think she crawled in there to take a nap with the calf." Wynne stood up and passed Hallee over the fence to Donna, then she opened the gate and went out.

"We've been looking all over for you, baby," Donna crooned. "Were you sleepy?"

Hallee yawned. "No." She held out her arms to Wynne, and Wynne took her back. Hallee twined her arms around her neck and snuggled against her shoulder. Wynne walked as quickly as she could toward the front of the barn, and Donna ran on ahead to alert the others.

As Wynne rounded the corner of the barn, Andrew met her, his face stony, and held out his arms for Hallee.

"I think she's asleep again," Wynne said. "She was having a nap in one of the hutches." Andrew put his arms around both of them and held them close with a huge sigh.

"I'll take her." He gently unwound Hallee's arms from Wynne's neck and cradled the little girl like an infant.

Hallee opened her eyes. "Daddy, is the hay unloaded?"

Andrew held her closer and kissed her sweaty forehead. "I've got a mind to paddle you."

Thomas and Irene came puffing around the corner, with Andy on their heels.

"Andrew, you've got her," Irene cried.

"There," Thomas said, smiling with satisfaction.

"Yes, I've got the little troublemaker." Andrew's scowl covered his relief.

His grandfather shook his head. "Now, son, she wasn't trying to be naughty."

"I know." Wynne thought a tear rolled down Andrew's cheek, but it might have been a bead of sweat.

Irene reached out her arms. "I'll take her in and put her in the bathtub. You'd best get at that last wagon. It's nearly lunchtime."

"All right, but take Wynne with you. She's done enough lifting today."

Wynne started to protest, but Andrew caught her eye and nodded sternly. He rubbed his cheek against Hallee's damp hair and set her down.

"Go on, almost-five-year-old." He swatted Hallee's backside. "You're big enough to walk to the bathtub."

Wynne hid her smile and went with Irene and Hallee to the house. She went upstairs for the little girl's clean clothes while Irene ran the bath water.

In Hallee's snug little room, she looked around. The single bed was covered with a bright log cabin quilt, with half a dozen stuffed animals grouped near the pillow, waiting for Hallee to play with them. On top of the pine dresser were a soft hairbrush, Hallee's ponytail holders, and a necklace of plastic pop beads.

She opened the drawers and lifted the little garments, choosing clean underpants, a striped T-shirt, and blue shorts.

Tears filled her eyes as she straightened. *Silly,* she told herself. *He's doing the right thing. Hallee and Andy will be fine, and you'll find someone else to fill your heart.*

"You look like you could use a bath yourself," Irene said when Wynne returned to the bathroom downstairs, the clean clothes over her arm. She was kneeling beside the bathtub, scrubbing Hallee's neck and arms with a washcloth.

"I think I'll go home and get one."

"Aren't you staying to lunch? Andrew expects you to stay." Irene squirted baby shampoo onto Hallee's hair.

Wynne eyed her doubtfully. "I'm so grubby! I don't think Andrew will miss me if I sneak out."

"He doesn't always say what he feels in words, but he does care, dear." Irene worked the shampoo into a lather.

Wynne couldn't hold the tears back. If she dared to think he really cared, things would be so much easier to bear. He had seemed concerned, at least, when he held her hand in the barnyard. They had become friends, but he was full of plans for moving his family, and she wasn't part of it.

She turned away, embarrassed to break down

in front of Irene and Hallee, and went out to the kitchen, where she found a box of tissues on the windowsill. She took one and blew her nose, gasping a little for breath. The screen door opened. Wynne stood with her back to the door.

"Everything all right?" Thomas asked.

"Yes, I think so." Wynne tried to speak cheerfully, but her voice broke a little. She dabbed at her eyes with a fresh tissue.

"Well, that's good."

She sensed Thomas hesitating, then the screen door opened and closed again. She looked over her shoulder cautiously, and found she was alone.

She knew Irene's kitchen well enough now to find a clean dishcloth and towel, and she took them to the sink and wet the cloth, then scrubbed her face and hands, washing her arms up to the elbows. As she patted her face dry, the door opened again, and she turned to face Andrew.

"Hi." He stood uncertainly in the doorway. "Are you okay?"

"Yes." She sniffed a little. "Are you?"

He nodded. "We're about done with the hay. Will you stay and eat with us?" He closed the screen quietly and walked slowly toward her.

Wynne held the damp towel up and wiped her forehead. Her hand shook.

"I—I thought I'd go home and get cleaned up. Maybe take a nap."

He leaned on the counter. "We worked you too hard this morning."

"No, really. It's just—the strain, I think. I was so scared when we couldn't find Hallee, and— I'll be all right, really." An errant tear spilled over, and she wiped it quickly away.

"Come here," he whispered and pulled her into his arms.

She sobbed then, burying her face in the front of his sweaty, smelly T-shirt. He stroked her hair, from the top of her head down to the end of her braid, then tightened both arms around her, and Wynne allowed herself to collapse against him.

The screen door opened again, and she stiffened, but Andrew held her firmly. The door closed softly, and when she turned her head toward it, no one was there.

"It's all right," Andrew said hoarsely. "It was just Grandpa."

She took a deep, ragged breath and slid her arms around him, locking her fingers behind his back.

"Now, tell me what's wrong," he said.

"Where do I start? There are so many things!"

"What's the worst thing?"

"I may have made a really big mistake this time."

"Tell me."

Wynne took a big breath. "I gave my notice at work yesterday."

He stood very still for a moment, and she could hear his heart beating rapidly.

"You're leaving?" he breathed near her ear.

"It looks like it. I was supposed to cover the murder trial that's starting Monday. I begged my boss to send someone else, but he wouldn't. He told me if I won't do it, I'm fired."

"Can they do that?"

"Yes."

"Isn't there a union?"

"Yes, but he says they'd have just cause because I wouldn't be fulfilling my contract."

"Okay. Well, it sounds like they win this round."

Wynne pulled away from him and looked up into gray-blue eyes that had never been so tender. "Andrew, it's the Pushard trial. Have you read the papers? The little girl was Hallee's age. I couldn't sit there and hear all the details without—" She sobbed, and he eased her gently back against his chest.

"I guess I missed that one. It's pretty bad, huh?"

"Horrible. At first I told Chuck I'd try, but I had to do some advance work yesterday, and it was terrible. Her stepfather is accused of—Andrew, I can't do it!"

He held her in silence for several seconds. Her heart pounded, but she drew comfort from his touch. At last he stroked her hair again. "I don't know what to tell you."

"You hated me from the first because of my job."

"No. I didn't hate you. I'm sorry I made you feel that way. I misjudged you, and I was out of line."

"Will you pray with me?"

"Of course." His voice was calm and steady as he brought her dilemma to the Lord. When he finished, Wynne found herself too choked up to pray aloud. "Thank you," she whispered.

"Will you get another job here?"

Wynne hesitated. "I haven't really had time to think about it. I had to give two weeks' notice, then I'll probably go home to my parents. I haven't told them yet."

"Why not?"

"I'm afraid they'll be disappointed."

"Nobody who loves you could want you to have to go to that trial if it bothers you so much."

"I feel guilty, and I know everyone will think I'm a failure."

"I won't. Because I know you want to do what's right."

She sighed. "A policeman told me I could do a lot of good by writing crime stories, but it tears me up inside. I couldn't sleep last night."

He was silent for a moment, his hands caressing her shoulders where the muscles ached with fatigue. "If it helps, I think you did the right thing. Maybe some people could do it without being affected so much, but for you, this is right."

Wynne's spirits lifted. "It does help, hearing you say that." He pulled her close again and held her silently, her head close to his heart.

After a few moments, he pushed her gently from him and rested his hands on her shoulders. "Go home, angel. Have a bath and get some clean clothes and a nap. I'll call you later and make sure you're not letting everything get you down."

She looked up at him, hating her nose that she knew was red, and her swollen eyes and her stringy, sweaty hair. "Thanks."

He bent his head and brushed her lips with his, then leaned back and looked deep into her eyes.

"Go now," he said softly.

She went without saying good-bye to Irene or Thomas. She couldn't stand to have them see her such a mess. The Turners were gone, and Will Boyer stood with Thomas beside the hay elevator, deep in conversation, while Andy sat lazily in the rim of one of the huge tractor wheels. She walked quickly to her car. In the rearview mirror, she saw Andrew amble toward his grandfather and join the debate.

Chapter 18

Irene's eyes brightened when Andrew came in for lunch the next Friday.

"Wynne called. She wants you to call her back at work."

He took the slip of paper from her hand and swallowed hard. He had sat next to Wynne at church on Sunday and had called her twice since the haying, drastic steps for a man emerging from five years of social apathy. Still, he felt he had just begun to get to know her.

His estimate of her character had shifted. He'd caught a few glimpses of her innermost fears and ambitions, and he knew she wasn't weak. The words he'd spoken to her on Saturday were true—not everyone was cut out to do every job.

The aversion he'd felt at their first meeting had been replaced by indifference, but that phase hadn't lasted long. Wynne had earned his grudging admiration, and finally his affection.

She was like him in many ways. Joyce had been his opposite, and he'd counted on her to jolly him out of depression. Wynne seemed to have a streak of melancholy as wide as his own, but she had a depth of sensitivity he'd never seen before, and a quiet courage he respected.

There was still so much he didn't know about

her. Every time he talked to her, some new aspect of her personality ambushed him. The positives far outnumbered the negatives now. It was terrifying, if he let himself think about it, so he tried not to. But that was a losing battle. He thought about her constantly.

With the telephone cord stretched to its limit, he retreated into the pantry for an illusion of privacy. The children were eagerly telling their grandmother about the new kittens in the equipment shed as he punched in the numbers.

She was so professional it threw him for a second. *"Waterville Guardian,* this is Wynne Harding speaking."

He wished he could see her bright eyes and the glossy dark hair that framed her face. Wished he could throw off the shyness that grabbed him and say easily, *Hello, angel.*

"Wynne? It's me."

He thought he heard a gentle sigh. "I'm glad you called. I had to type a notice about a new business in Augusta."

"Oh?"

"I thought there might be a job there."

"For you?"

"No, for *you.*"

His mind raced. He wasn't sure he liked this, taking tips for job hunting from the woman to whom he was so attracted. On the other hand, without a job, he wasn't in a very good position to pursue a romantic relationship. He decided he would take any help he could get.

"Andrew, there's a commuter company coming into the airport. They're planning scheduled flights to Bangor, Portland, and Boston. Maybe more later on."

His pulse picked up. "They haven't had commercial service from Augusta in years."

"That's what the press release said. I don't know if it means anything or not, but . . . I could give you the contact number. They're based in Portland."

When he'd hung up, he took a deep breath and hit the buttons for the number she'd given him. No sense waiting and hoping. Better to find out quickly if there was an opportunity for him.

As the ringing began, he wished he'd talked to her longer. A curt *thanks* was all he'd mustered, when he wanted to say so much more.

After the evening milking, Andrew showered and ate quickly. He considered calling Wynne but decided it would be much more satisfactory to talk to her in person. Still, he wasn't ready when she opened the door of the little rental house, her eyes wide. She was wearing a green sleeveless dress, and waves of chestnut hair shimmered over her shoulders.

Andrew swallowed hard. "You're beautiful."

Her dark eyes flared and her cheeks reddened,

but she smiled, and he felt he'd made an inane understatement.

"Thank you." Her lip trembled just a bit, and she stood there waiting.

He looked down at his sneakers. "I'm sorry. I just wanted to tell you I'm going for an interview next week."

"Really? They need pilots?"

"They're considering hiring one more person on this end. I'd have to go for some training and lock in my commercial license, but it shouldn't take more than two or three months and—well, we'll have enough money from the farm, after we buy a house."

She nodded, and he allowed himself a long look into her eyes. Amazing how she could send his common sense packing without saying a word.

"It might not all work out," he said, "but even so, it's the best thing I've heard about yet. If I go through all that and they don't hire me, I'll at least be qualified to apply at some other small airline. So, thanks."

"You're welcome. So . . . you'd look at houses in the area?"

"Yeah. Grandma's already talked to a real estate agent. We plan to start looking next week. And, hey . . . I read Deedee Rollins's story about the trial today."

"What did you think?"

He gritted his teeth. "I'm glad you didn't have to go."

"Me too. Now that I've made the decision, it's a relief." She smiled shakily. "Guess I need to call my parents."

"You still haven't told them?"

"Not yet. How does this sound? 'Mom, Dad, I'm looking at the classifieds for the New Hampshire papers. Oh, and is my room still vacant?' "

He chuckled. "Better just be straight with them."

"You're probably right. I'm having a yard sale tomorrow."

"What for?"

"I have to sell most of my furniture. Oh, I won't sell the dresser. Could you come and get it next week? I know Irene will protest, but I can't take it in my car."

He ran a hand through his hair. It was so final. Something inside him wanted to scream, *Don't go!* But his brain said calmly, *You have no job. You have two children. Your life is impossibly complicated, and you hardly know her.*

"What about your sister?"

"Rebecca doesn't want me to go. She and Rob said I can stay with them for a while if I want to look for another job up here."

He looked at his truck, then back at her. "Wynne—" They stared at each other for a long moment. His pulse hammered. She ought to be able to hear it, and to feel the longing he couldn't express.

"I—I just don't feel like I should intrude on them," she said. "Rebecca just found out she's expecting, and—"

"Hey, that's great."

"Yes, but . . . Will you write to me if I go, and tell me how the job situation turns out?" she whispered, edging back in the doorway.

His heart sank. "Sure."

"I'll give you the address on Sunday."

He closed his eyes and took a deep breath. When he opened them, she was closing the door, her eyes large and miserable.

"Wynne, don't—" He flung out his arm and stopped the door from closing the last six inches.

She blinked.

"Look, I'm going for the interview next Friday. Can I come see you after?"

Two tears spilled over as she nodded. "That's my last day at the paper."

He lowered his arm, and she closed the door slowly.

He dragged his feet as he walked to the pickup. He should have kissed her. He should have told her he loved her. Begged her to stay. He stood uncertainly for a moment looking at the house, then he got in the truck. Nothing had changed.

His life was still in chaos. He had a week before she left.

Please, Lord, don't take her away from me and the kids. Give me the right to ask her to stay.

Chuck kept her working hard all week, pushing her to the edge of exhaustion. She missed the Bible study Wednesday evening to cover a city council meeting. Each night, she fell into bed too tired to agonize over the impending separation from Andrew. If he'd only said *stay* . . .

On Thursday, she interviewed three school board members by phone and went out to an automobile accident with Ken. The cars had been towed before they got there, and the ambulance was long gone, so she had to call the state police and get the story from their spokesman.

That afternoon she went to the park and interviewed the foreman of the crew remodeling the playground. When she got back to the office, she found a stack of phone messages on her desk and began methodically returning calls.

As she typed away at the playground story, panic began to rise. Her throat seemed to close, and each breath was a struggle. She was nearing deadline, and the story was going slowly. Around her, computer keys clacked, conversation hummed, and the scanner chattered intermittently.

Her eyes snapped open as she heard, "Barton Road, Belgrade."

"Did they say Barton Road?"

Julie looked up from her keyboard. "Didn't hear it."

Wynne got up and walked quickly toward Chuck's desk, where the scanner sat on a shelf.

"Fire departments in Belgrade, Oakland, Sidney and Rome, structure fire on Barton Road, Belgrade."

She hurried back to her desk and grabbed her purse. Chuck was entering the room with a cup of coffee in his hand.

"There's a fire in Belgrade. I'm going out there."

"Do you need a photographer?"

"Yes."

"I'll go." Ken was at her side.

Chuck nodded. "All right, make it good. I'll pull something from page one."

Her hands were almost numb as she clutched the steering wheel, and she relaxed them with great effort, breathing rapidly as she drove toward the Cooks' home, sending up a constant stream of prayers.

She saw the smoke in the sky halfway between Oakland and Belgrade, and when she topped the hill beyond the church, the black cloud stood like a towering tree on the skyline.

"That's got to be something big." Ken was preparing his camera while she drove. "Isn't this where we came when the little girl got hurt?"

"I'm praying it's not them."

She turned onto Barton Road and sped up. As she got closer to the Cooks', the smoke was still distant, and she began to hope that the fire was beyond their property. She turned in at the driveway and stopped her car between the tranquil house and barn.

"This will just take a second, Ken." She breathed deeply and prayed, *Thank You, Lord! Thank You.*

Irene came out from the kitchen, and Andy and Hallee raced past her, reaching the car as Wynne opened the door. The smell of smoke filled her nostrils.

"Nana and Grandpa Turner's barn is on fire," Hallee wailed, and Wynne gathered her and Andy in her arms, looking past them to Irene.

"The fire is at the Turners'?"

"Yes, their hay barn. As far as I know it hasn't spread, but—"

Two fire trucks went screaming by, and the rest of Irene's words were lost.

"Daddy and Grandpa went down to help." Andy's pride was tempered with wistfulness and perhaps a smidgen of fear.

"Donna called here right after they called the fire department." Irene looked anxiously toward the smoke-filled sky. "They asked for the men to come help them move the stock out into the farthest pasture, away from the buildings, and try to save their equipment."

"The photographer and I are going down there," Wynne said. "Keep praying. I'll get you word as soon as I can."

A ladder truck and an ambulance whizzed past, sirens blaring. Wynne and Irene looked at each other in dismay.

"That was an Oakland truck," said Irene.

"The ambulance—"

"Probably routine. Still—" Irene sounded less confident than Wynne would have liked.

"I'm going. Take the children inside."

Wynne drove out to the roadway and turned toward the Turners' farm. The smoke grew thicker as she advanced half a mile, to where a police officer made her stop. Cars and trucks lined the road from that point to the Turners' driveway.

"You can't go down there. You can turn around in that driveway over there." The officer gestured toward a mailbox across the road.

"We're here for the paper."

"You'll get in the way of the firemen, miss. You need to turn around and get out of the way and go somewhere and wait for news."

Wynne looked questioningly at Ken.

"Park here. We'll walk."

Wynne threw her car into reverse and backed up until she could pull to the side of the road behind a pickup. She and Ken walked rapidly along the row of cars. The stench of smoke increased, and she brushed bits of ash from her pants.

Wynne spotted a familiar figure at the end of the farm's long driveway and began to run toward it.

"Dave! Dave Workman!"

He turned toward her. "Well, it's Lois Lane! You here for the story?"

"Yes. What's happening?"

"Well, the family's got their hands full." He took his hat off for a moment and wiped his forehead.

"Is everyone all right? We saw the ambulance."

"I think so. Hold on." A tank truck was lumbering down the road, its piercing siren growing louder, then abruptly going silent as Dave waved the driver into the farm lane. Wynne took her hands from over her ears and waited until the truck passed.

"Let me check with the unit that's up there." Dave spoke into his portable radio, and a crackly noise came from it. "Any casualties?" he asked, and the radio crackled again. Wynne didn't recognize the sounds as words, but apparently Dave did.

"No one hurt," he told her. "The ambulance was standard backup. Sometimes they'll get a fireman who needs oxygen or something."

Visions of Andrew and Thomas inhaling the

choking, thick smoke sprang to her mind. "We're going up there."

Dave winked at her. "I'm supposed to keep people like you away. Keep out from underfoot, Lois."

"We will."

Another fire truck approached, and Dave turned toward it. Ken was already walking rapidly up the driveway, and Wynne raced after him.

Chapter 19

The sun was sinking low, and the smoke made the sky darker than it should have been. Bits of ash fell all around Wynne, like snow. At least six fire trucks sat in the yard, and a tanker lumbered past her, heading out to refill at the farm pond down the road.

Flames still flared from the hay barn. The loft and most of the roof had collapsed, and huge mounds of baled hay inside were burning. Firemen hosed the side and roof of another barn. The house, set a little apart, seemed unharmed. A knot of adults and children stood near the side of the house, and Wynne strode toward them.

"Judy!"

Pete's wife turned toward her, and her face lit in recognition.

"Wynne."

"Is everyone all right?"

"Yes, we're fine. It's the hay barn."

Ken drifted toward the conflagration, adjusting his camera settings.

"What happened?" Wynne asked.

"We don't know," Judy replied. "It could be spontaneous combustion, if the hay wasn't dry enough."

"You're the reporter," another young woman

said. She was obviously pregnant, and a three-year-old clung to her hand.

"This is Mary Ann, Bob Junior's wife," Judy said. "This is Wynne Harding."

"Andrew's new girlfriend." Mary Ann looked her up and down.

"Oh, please," said Wynne, "I'm not—"

"It's all right," Judy said with a smile. "You've passed muster with Donna and me, and we've been telling Mom Turner you're what Andrew needs."

"But we're not—I mean—"

Donna came and stood beside her. "The look on Andrew's face says you are."

Judy nodded. "He's always been quiet, but when he came around here to see Joyce, you could tell he was serious."

"Deadly serious," said Donna.

"He had the same look that day, when you found Hallee," Judy said.

Wynne felt the blood rushing to her cheeks.

"You guys are jumping to conclusions," Mary Ann said to her sisters-in-law.

"Miss Harding, isn't it?" Helen Turner was approaching, eyeing Wynne coolly. Wearing blue slacks and a *Country Woman* T-shirt, she seemed less intimidating than she had in the cemetery.

"Yes, ma'am," Wynne replied. "I'm here for the *Guardian*."

"Well, the men got all the stock out, in case the

fire spreads. We've lost our hay barn and three thousand bales of hay, and a manure spreader. That's all I know about so far."

Wynne scribbled hastily in her notebook. Smoke rose from the blackened heaps of baled hay, and flames erupted sporadically. The firemen continued to pour water onto the smoldering ruins.

"Thomas and Andrew got here quickly, and they helped move all the cattle out in time." Helen caught her breath.

Wynne turned toward the barn. They all watched anxiously as another part of its roof caved in.

Standing with the Turner women, Wynne waited for a lull when she could get some information from the fire chief. Ken was getting as close to the fire as he could, snapping pictures.

"Irene was pretty worried. I'd better call her." She pulled her cell phone from her pocket.

"I should have thought to call Irene back," Judy said. "Tell her everyone's safe, okay?"

Wynne placed the call, assuring Irene that no one was injured. While she stood watching the tank trucks come and go, she was introduced to several of Andrew's nieces and nephews.

Helen was watching her. Wynne felt she was on display, although Judy and Donna treated her as a friend.

"Could I speak to you?" Helen asked, coming closer.

"Of course." Wynne tried not to stutter.

They stepped away from the others, nearer the house.

"I'm sorry this happened," Wynne said.

"Thank you. I just wanted to tell you that Andrew came to see me a couple of days ago. I didn't know if you knew."

"No, he didn't mention it to me." Wynne's apprehension activated. She was sweating, and it wasn't from the heat of the fire.

"He came to tell me that he's fallen in love. He was apologetic. I think he was afraid Bob and I would be upset."

Wynne lowered her eyes, her heart racing.

"Bob and I don't have any hard feelings toward Andrew. What happened to Joyce was very difficult, but it wasn't his fault. He's done a good job with the children, and it wouldn't upset me to see him remarry. It's been five years, and I know it's been hard for him. He deserves another chance."

"Thank you," Wynne whispered.

Helen smiled. "We'll be sorry if he and the children move away, but it will be some consolation if the children have a mother who loves them."

"I *do* love them, Mrs. Turner."

Helen looked hard at her for a moment, then

nodded. "We would write and send cards and gifts. You wouldn't mind?"

Wynne flushed. "We're not engaged or anything, Mrs. Turner, but I'm sure Andrew would want that. They're your grandchildren, and I know they love you and your husband."

Helen nodded and smiled.

They walked slowly back to where Helen's daughters-in-law waited. Wynne saw one of the fire captains walking toward a tanker, and she hurried to get a few words with him. With a few strategic questions she had enough information for the story, and she looked around anxiously for Ken.

Several men came from behind the second barn. Wynne scanned their faces and spotted Thomas and Andrew among the Turner men.

"Wynne!" Andrew stopped walking, and she ran past the other men to him. Smiling, he opened his arms, and she flew into them. The smoky smell was strong on his shirt, but she clung to him for a few seconds.

Thomas waited until Andrew released her and then came close. "Are you here on business, dear?"

"Yes, the paper sent me. Are you all right?" She dashed away a tear with the back of her hand.

"We're fine."

Andrew kept his arm around her and squeezed

her shoulder. "Looks like things are under control here."

"Thank you, Tom," Bob Turner called as they walked slowly toward the driveway. He came over and pumped Thomas's hand. "You, too, Andrew. Don't know as we'd have gotten all the young stock out without you."

"Thank God they contained the fire," Thomas said.

"Yes, it's a big loss, but it could have been much worse," Bob replied.

"Well, if there's anything more we can do, holler." Thomas pulled a bandanna from the pocket of his overalls and wiped his brow.

"Would you say something for the *Guardian*, Mr. Turner?" Wynne asked, holding her pen and notebook ready.

"Our neighbors are God's blessing to us. Without them . . ." He shook his head. "We'll have to assess the damage tomorrow. I can tell you right now, we'll be looking for more hay fields to cut."

"You'll get a good second cut off our place," Thomas told him. "Might be more than you need for the cattle Pete's getting from us."

Wynne finished her writing and pocketed the notebook. "Thank you. I know this is a stressful time to be talking to the press."

"Where's your car?" Andrew asked her.

"Down the road about half a mile. The cops stopped us there."

"My truck's right here. We'll drive you down to your car."

"Ken's with me." She saw the photographer approaching and waved to him. "We've got a ride."

She slid into the cab of the pickup, between Andrew and Thomas, and Ken hopped in the back. The Turner family waved as Andrew drove slowly toward the road, waiting to let another tanker up the driveway.

"We got there before the first fire truck," Thomas said. "Looked like it started in the hay mow. The roof was all smoking on the south side. Henry spotted it when he went out to start milking. Couldn't believe it at first. Thought it was mist or something."

Andrew eased the truck out onto the hardtop. "They were chasing the cows out of the free stall barn when we got there. We got all the young stock out, too, and drove them down to the lower pasture where they couldn't possibly be hurt."

"Thank God the house didn't burn," said Wynne.

"Oh, yes," Thomas agreed. "Things could have been a whole lot worse, considering."

"That young stock barn would have gone if it didn't have a steel roof." Andrew shook his head. "Good thing we got the critters out. It got pretty hot in there." He glanced over at Thomas. "Think this will change things as far as them buying the farm?"

"I don't think so," said Thomas. "Pete wants to go ahead with the deal."

"The Turners are buying your farm?" Wynne stared at Andrew, then Thomas. They were really moving away, then, and probably soon.

"That's the plan." Andrew looked over at her, and his crooked smile was reassuring. "Pete's wanted to buy it for a long time."

Thomas rolled down the window. "They've got insurance. I expect the sale will go forward."

They reached her car, and Thomas let Wynne out. Smoke was still heavy in the air, but not nearly so bad as it had been in the Turners' yard. Ken joined her for the ride back to the office. She waved at Andrew as she backed carefully out from between two trucks and turned around in the driveway the policeman had pointed out earlier.

She began to mentally compose her story about the fire while she drove the ten miles to Waterville. Her thoughts frequently went racing off at the memory of Andrew's touch and his obvious pleasure in seeing her. And Helen's words sprang into her thoughts. *He came to tell me that he's fallen in love.*

"What are you grinning about?" Ken asked. "Your friends just had a huge fire."

She tried, but she couldn't repress the smile. "Tomorrow's my last day at the office."

"Oh, right. We'll miss you, kiddo."

The next day, Wynne found the book she had loaned Julie lying on her desk. She turned and looked across the aisle at her friend.

"Are you done with this?"

"Yes, I finished it."

"So? What did you think?"

Julie glanced around at the busy newsroom. "Come in the library for a sec." She got up and walked away.

Wynne looked after her, then rose and followed. Julie was waiting for her near the file cabinets that comprised the morgue.

"If it's all true," Julie began, "well, if it is, then I need to do something about it."

Wynne nodded. "It's true, Julie."

"So, what do I do?"

"Believe it."

Julie hesitated. "What if I believe it and it's not true?"

Wynne cocked her head a little to one side. "If you're still not sure it's true, then I guess you're not believing it."

"But what if I truly, whole-heartedly believe it, and I find out later it's not? Like when I die?"

"What would you lose?"

Julie frowned. "There's something strange about that reasoning."

"So, do you believe it?"

"I'm not sure. Part of me wants to. The other part says, *Run! This woman is crazy!*"

"Come to church with me Sunday," Wynne said.

"Oh, I don't know. I've never been to church."

"Since when have you been afraid to try something new?"

Julie's face contorted. "Since my brother talked me into riding a steer at my grandfather's farm. I broke my wrist."

"When was this?"

"Twelve years ago."

Wynne smiled. "I'm not giving up on you."

"I'll think about it."

Wynne went back to work, determined to be productive even on her last day. She was typing rapidly as quitting time neared, concentrating on her article, when something floated past her nose. She jumped and stared at the paper airplane that had settled on the desktop beyond the computer. She whipped around toward the doorway.

Andrew stood watching her. In an instant she noted his neat gray suit and stylish necktie, his gleaming shoes, and most of all, his huge grin.

"What's this?"

"Airmail." His voice was just loud enough for her to hear him, but even so, several heads lifted.

Wynne glanced toward the paper airplane again and saw that something was printed on it in blue ink. She stretched to retrieve it and opened the wings slowly.

Come out to the farm for supper?

She smiled and nodded. Andrew gave her a thumb's up and turned toward the elevator.

"That guy looks familiar." Julie was smiling speculatively at Wynne.

"Who is he?" asked Esther.

Light dawned on Julie's face. "Isn't he your farmer friend?"

"Pretty snappy dresser for a farmer," Esther said.

Wynne smiled. "Actually, I think he's an airline pilot."

"He's cute," said Deedee, hardly pausing in her typing.

"He can fly me anywhere he wants." Esther turned back to her monitor.

Wynne tried to concentrate on her work, but the comments bounced around her.

"Who are we talking about?" Scott called.

Deedee made a face. "Wynne's new boyfriend."

"Is that why you're leaving?" Scott asked.

"What do you care?" asked Julie.

"I was thinking about asking Wynne out."

Julie scowled at him. "You should have thought of that a month ago."

Esther raised her eyebrows. "You can't compete with the fly boy."

"You wouldn't stand a chance," Deedee agreed.

Chapter 20

When she arrived at the farm, Andrew came out to meet her. He was dressed once more in jeans and a faded blue T-shirt, and he looked almost boyish as he came eagerly toward her. The girls were right, Wynne thought. No one could compete with that smile.

"You got the job."

He slid his arms around her. "Thanks to you. I'll be going for six weeks of training on their jets. And my license should be all set when I finish that."

"I'm so happy!" She hugged him quickly, but when she moved away, he held on.

"We need to talk."

"Now?"

"Later." He planted a soft kiss just in front of her ear. "A.T.B."

She raised her eyebrows.

"After the twin's bedtime."

She laughed.

Andy and Hallee ran out the kitchen door, making a beeline for Wynne.

"Miss Harding!" Hallee leaped into her arms. "Our daddy got a new job!"

"I know, sweetheart. It's wonderful."

Andy tugged at her sleeve, and Wynne bent toward him.

"He's going to fly flugzeugs."

She pulled Andy toward her and embraced both children. "Maybe sometime we can get a ride," she whispered.

Hallee scowled. "He has to go away to airplane school, though."

"Just for a few weeks," Andrew said, "and I can come home every weekend."

Irene peered out the screen door. "Come right in, Wynne. Supper's ready."

Andrew reached for Wynne's hand and walked with her. Hallee wouldn't let go of her other hand, and Andy walked beside his father.

Irene and Thomas greeted her with a suppressed excitement. The twins continued to chatter through the meal and cleanup time. They all sat in the living room afterward, and Andrew told them about his trip to Portland, the interview, and the details of his training and new job.

"We'll have to start a new album." Thomas leaned back in his recliner, clearly happy. "Captain Cook. You're starting a dynasty of explorers now."

"Well, don't expect me to name any kids Christopher Columbus or Ferdinand Magellan," Andrew said testily, but he smiled at Wynne.

"Well, I, for one, am tired," said Irene. "These little ones ought to be in bed, I know that."

"Yup. Come on, pardner." Andrew slapped Andy on the thigh and stood up. "I'll tuck you in. Let's go." He looked back over his shoulder at Wynne. "Don't go away."

She smiled and nodded.

"Carry me, Daddy," Hallee pleaded.

"You're spoiled rotten." Andrew picked her up and headed for the stairs. "You got rocks in your pockets? You're heavy."

"What rhymes with heavy?" Hallee asked.

"Chevy," Andrew said.

"Levee," Andy chimed in from the step behind them.

"That's not a word," Hallee protested.

"Oh, yes it is." Her father kept going.

"Daddy," Andy said, "what did the angel cook for Gideon?"

They were out of earshot before Andrew replied.

"I'm surprised he remembered that." Wynne arched her eyebrows at Irene.

"He's a serious little tyke, like his father was. He's probably been thinking about it for weeks. That, or Thomas has been singing it in the barn." Irene smiled at Wynne. "We're so happy about this."

"You mean Andrew's new job?" she asked in confusion.

"Yes. He's been so discouraged. And now . . ."

"Now we can move forward," Thomas said.

"You'll all stay together, won't you?"

Irene's lips trembled. "I don't think we could bear to be separated from those little ones after all this time."

"They'd be lost without you."

Thomas watched Wynne with his twinkling blue eyes and irrepressible smile. "The boy's made it clear he wants us to stay with him. No old folks' home for us, eh, Irene?"

"I'm glad," Wynne said.

Irene stood up and walked to the mantel. She picked up the photograph of Andrew in his Air Force uniform. "I'll try not to worry about him when he's flying."

Thomas shook his head. "Worrying doesn't do any good. Anyway, he's a good pilot. His Air Force flight instructor gave him a terrific reference."

Andrew came back down the stairs, and Thomas stood. "Good night, Wynne. I expect we'll see you Sunday."

She stood up hastily and kissed his wrinkled cheek. "Good night." She turned to embrace Irene. "Thank you for having me."

Andrew nodded toward the kitchen and beyond. "Stroll down to the brook?"

As she walked beside him in the darkening twilight, she reveled in his nearness. A breeze was coming up, relieving the heat of the day. It ruffled Wynne's hair, and she turned her face toward it, catching a faint whiff of the acrid smoke that had hung in the air the night before.

Andrew reached for her hand, and she clung to his without looking at him. If she did, he would see her intense love, and she wasn't sure the time was right for that.

They climbed up and sat once more on the rock beside the stream.

"Grandpa and I looked at a place Wednesday." Andrew hefted a pebble and tossed it into the water below.

"A place? What kind of place?"

"It's an old farmhouse, down in Winthrop. They've sold off most of the land, but it has about ten acres."

"Enough for a nice, big garden." She mentally calculated the mileage between Belgrade and Winthrop.

"And maybe a pony or two. It's only eight miles from the airport." When he turned toward her, his eyes gleamed. "It would be big enough for—for the family. And there's a first-floor bedroom for Gramp and Grammy."

"I'm glad your grandparents have decided to stay with you."

"I insisted." He was watching her closely, and she smiled up at him, her pulse galloping.

"It would be awful to be separated from them now."

"Do you think so? Because they can be a little stubborn at times. Especially Grandpa."

She laughed. "And you can't?"

The moon had topped the trees along the stream. Andrew inched closer to her on the rock, and she raised her eyes to his. As he bent toward her, a tiny twinge of the old anxiety sharpened the hope that had begun to replace it. Wynne put her hand on his shoulder to steady herself and fleetingly wondered what would happen if they fell from the rock into the brook below.

Andrew eased his arms around her, and she clasped her hands behind his neck. He buried his face in her hair, and they sat silent, savoring the perfection of the moment.

"Wynne, I love you."

She sighed deeply and nestled her head on his shoulder. "I love you, too." The relief of saying it at last was enormous. He tipped her face toward him and kissed her, long and sweet.

"Don't go, Wynne. That's what I wanted to tell you last week. I can't stand it if you leave."

A rush of joy and dismay ran through her. She put her hand gently to his cheek and traced the line of his scratchy jaw with her index finger. "My parents told me to come home, but Rebecca and Rob are looking for a job for me up here. My dad offered to try to line up something for me in New Hampshire, but I told him I really don't want to leave Maine again."

"What about your rental house?"

"I gave it up, as of next Saturday."

His arms tightened around her. "Stay. Please. We need you. *I* need you. I'll make your dad understand." He kissed her again, and she knew her objections were meaningless.

"Wynne, will you marry me? I want you to be my wife, and a mother for Hallee and Andy." He looked searchingly into her eyes.

She closed them for an instant as she caught her breath. "Yes. There's nothing I want more."

He smiled and exhaled slowly, drew her close again, and kissed her tenderly. "There's one more thing, to make it official." He reached in his pocket and held out a small box. "Grandma gave me this when I got home today."

Wynne opened it and saw a diamond ring glittering in the moonlight. No wonder Irene and Thomas were so keyed up tonight.

"Your mother's?" she guessed.

"No, Chet's wife has Mom's. This is Grandma's. She said she's too plump to wear it now, and she'd like you to have it if you want it." He added hastily, "If you'd rather have a new one, that's all right, but—"

"Of course I want it! I'd love to wear Irene's ring."

He pulled her to his chest and sighed in contentment.

After a moment she turned slightly to lean

against him and took the ring from the box. "Let's see if it fits."

Andrew lifted her left hand and slid the band gently onto her third finger. "Pretty close, I think."

"I think so, too." Wynne smiled up at him. He kissed her again, and her heart soared. This was perfect, this was right. She had no misgivings, no latent regrets or longings, no unfulfilled hopes. She knew her relationship with Andrew would change, but the thought held no fear now. As she learned to know him better, they would only grow closer.

He released her and sat watching her. Even though there was no tension in his posture, she sensed a fire beneath his complacence.

"Guess I need to send you home," he said softly. He put his finger to her lips and lightly traced their curve.

Wynne closed her eyes for an instant, enjoying the new ease she felt with his nearness. When she opened them, he was smiling, and a thrill of realization shot through her. She would be his wife soon.

"It's getting late," she agreed.

He climbed carefully down from the rock and held up both arms. Wynne hopped down lightly, and he held her for a long moment before they turned to walk back up the path. The farmhouse was dark.

He walked with her to her car and turned her toward him. He kissed her lingeringly in the moonlight, and whispered in her ear, "I don't exactly know how to say this, but if there's anything you want to know about Joyce, just ask. I love you, and I don't want any awkwardness between us."

Wynne swallowed hard. She didn't think she wanted to know the details of his first marriage, but there was one thing that had been nagging at her. She rested her hands lightly on his shoulders, and the diamond caught a ray of moonlight and winked at her, giving her courage. "There's nothing big, but I hope you won't be making comparisons, because I don't think I'm very like Joyce."

"No, you're not like her at all."

"Well, I know you loved her, and that's all right. I'd be upset if you didn't. But it scares me a little to think you might expect me to do things the way she did, or—"

"Don't worry about that," he whispered, kissing her temple. "I love you the way you are."

She clung to him, her head against his warm shoulder.

"Anything else?" he asked softly.

"Will you go to Rebecca and Rob's with me tomorrow? They invited me for lunch. I know you have a lot going on, but—"

"I think I can get away."

"Great. I'll call her when I get home and tell her to expect both of us. And . . . just for the record, would you consider naming a child Henry Hudson Cook or Richard Byrd Cook?"

He pulled her in for another kiss.

About the Author

Susan Page Davis is the author of more than one hundred published novels. She's a two-time winner of the Inspirational Readers' Choice Award and the Will Rogers Medallion, and also a winner of the Carol Award and a finalist in the WILLA Literary Awards. A Maine native, she now lives in Kentucky. Visit her website at: https://susanpagedavis.com, where you can see all her books, sign up for her occasional newsletter, and read fun features on her "Freebies" tab. If you liked this book, please consider writing a review and posting it on Amazon, Goodreads, or the venue of your choice.

Find Susan at:

Website: https://susanpagedavis.com
Amazon: https://www.amazon.com/Susan
-Page-Davis/e/B001IR1CGA
BookBub: https://www.bookbub.com/authors
/susan-page-davis
Twitter: @SusanPageDavis
Facebook: https://www.facebook.com
/susanpagedavisauthor

Center Point Large Print
600 Brooks Road / PO Box 1
Thorndike, ME 04986-0001 USA

(207) 568-3717

US & Canada:
1 800 929-9108
www.centerpointlargeprint.com